Writing Love

Writing Love

Khalil Sweileh

—◁◁—

Translated by
Alexa Firat

The American University in Cairo Press
Cairo   New York

First published in 2012 by
The American University in Cairo Press
113 Sharia Kasr el Aini, Cairo, Egypt
www.aucpress.com

Dar el Kutub No. 11220/11
ISBN 978 977 416 535 1

Dar el Kutub Cataloging-in-Publication Data

Sweileh, Khalil
        Writing Love/ Khalil Sweileh. —Cairo: The American University
    in Cairo Press, 2012
            p.   cm.
        ISBN 978 977 416 535 1
        1. Love in Literature   2. Love in Arabic literature
        I. Title
        892.70803543

1 2 3 4 5   16 15 14 13 12

Designed by Andrea El-Akshar
Printed in Egypt

I rarely like other people's novels. I especially dislike those weighted down by history and wars, as if they were meant to wreak havoc on the readers' psyche. I have become quite an expert at discovering bad novels based on their covers, the name of the writer, or even the title. When I tour bookstores, a quick glance is enough to know whether I should bother reading a novel or not. By the way, I can also smell it.

I admit it, I am not a novelist. However, I have been seduced by the notion of writing a novel that can drag a reader by the ears into its private hell. My ability to write rests confidently on a long association of 'friends,' that is, novelists. It is as if the texts that I read and scrutinize, even editing some of their sentences with my red, black, and fluorescent green highlighter pens, were written just for me. Written to spread joy in my damaged soul, they set the same traps for me time and again. Right now,

I am sure that I could call out to the spirits of dozens of characters whose shadows hover over me. We know each other well. We have met before in other places and at different times, and sometimes exchange secret, cryptic letters that restore a semblance of balance to my fragile existence.

At this moment, I am trying to glean the first seeds that led me to think, foolishly, of writing this so-called novel. They came out of nowhere one wintry afternoon while I was poring over the pages of *The History of Reading* by a writer I had never heard of before, Alberto Manguel. (Perhaps he's Argentinean.) "Reading, like breathing, is a necessity of life," is written on the back cover. This author set out to follow the vestiges of texts, as they are written, read, and printed across different historical periods. I think the thing that drew me to this work was his relationship with one of my most beloved writers, Jorges Luis Borges. Miguel spent two entire years reading him, day after day, blind to the rest of the world, and it was sections from *A Thousand and One Nights* that reverberated with him the most.

That night I left my house as usual, aimlessly walking familiar streets for some air and a look at the brightly lit storefronts. I stopped in at Maysalun Bookstore. I found a lot of books there, although nothing recent on the war in Afghanistan or Osama bin Laden. I thought for a moment that the reason I was thinking about writing a novel that could summarize all the novels I had read over the past thirty years was because it was a way for me to ward off the stench emanating from America's dirty war. A war launched a number of years ago against a miserable and hungry people, each insolent act captivating the world and wiping out everyone's individuality.

Sitting in a café, my mind was preoccupied with finding the key, the cipher to this novel. I thought about starting it with a description of the protagonist's visit to a corner of old Damascus, following in the footsteps of novelists enamored with their local environment. His path would lead him to the Umayyad Mosque in search of some writing on the walls that he would record in a notebook. Here, the first amorphous idea would pop into the narrator's head (who, at this time, is the protagonist of the novel), that is, to collect primary material on the history of writing, such as maxims and proverbs engraved on the doors of old houses, walls, and archways, and use them as reference points to shape the connective tissue of the narrative. Expressions like, "A blessed Hajj, a praised ritual"; "Sovereignty belongs to God"; or "In the name of God, the merciful and compassionate."

In order not to fall into a rhetorical snarl, I have decided, from this line on, to narrate what is happening by way of the narrator's voice, like a kind of autobiography that I think is quite enticing to readers, especially if I blend it with some intriguing confessions. This is what I am working out for you in the following sections. Perhaps it will happen on page ninety-eight (and I chose this number as a good omen because of what my friend Henry Miller did in *Tropic of Capricorn*). Indeed, I gave this novel as a present to a colleague at work a few years ago, jotting a clever note on the inside cover: "The most beautiful novels are those that are read from page 98 onward, especially this one." However, my plan to woo her failed completely. Now, I could have rewritten reality by claiming that my quest for her was a success. But the truth of the matter is that when I met her in the elevator the next day and tried to kiss her in an attempt to condense time and space (I was sure that she had caught my drift), she slapped me quite hard. Then she pulled the book out of her bag and shoved it in my face, storming out of the elevator.

After my spiritual tour of the Umayyad Mosque, I headed down a few steps toward al-Nawfara Café. I ordered a mint tea like any nameless novelist deluded into thinking that his omission from the Nobel laureate list was a mistake. The storyteller at this famed café presented an opportunity to uncover another 'key' to the novel, to benefit from the storyteller's narrative method. I decided to procure copies of famous classical biographies, like those of Antara, al-Zahir Baybars, and Abu Zayd al-Hilali, and to select sections of them to put in the novel itself or perhaps to imitate their style. Then, while admiring the antique wooden balconies hanging over the café, I thought of a new entryway for the novel that was much better than the other ones. Thinking

4

about this one got me so excited I started shaking. A trader from Baghdad sets out to find a khan for the night to rest after much heavy traveling. While passing through one of the alleyways, he notices an incredibly beautiful woman peeking out from behind a screened balcony. He is filled with a familiar anxiety. Finding a khan nearby he asks the owner about this woman, who tells him that the house has been abandoned for at least a year. The whole thing grows even wilder and more transcendent in his mind. The next morning he wakes up disoriented and anxious—he had seen her in his dream just as he had seen her the day before. Upon leaving the khan, he heads for the café across from the house with the balcony to see her with his own eyes. And there he sits for seven nights, neither a drop of food nor water passing his lips. The caravan that he came with leaves without him. At the end of the seventh night, he slips into the house and finds it vacant just as the owner of the khan had claimed. In the courtyard he finds a box that must have been left behind. After some trepidation he opens it, only to find a scrap of paper that reads, "If you want me to be your spouse and wish to pay my dowry, then you must transcribe for me a book that contains the most beautiful things said about love, separation, and death."

So, after an absence of nineteen years, seven months, and thirteen days this man was found dead at the doorstep of the house. The alleyway was blocked by a caravan of camels carrying hundreds of manuscripts that he had collected throughout his long journeys in which he wandered between Persia, the Caucasus, Andalusia, Fez, Cairo, Baghdad, and Jerusalem, finally arriving at Damascus in the beginning of the month Dhu al-Qaʿda in the year AH 237. A passerby found him sprawled on the ground and realized as he approached that he was dead. A scrap of paper next to the body caught his attention. He read it and was amazed by what he learned about this stranger:

> In the name of God the compassionate and merciful . . . From Abdullah Zayd ibn Ibrahim al-Baghdadi to Yasmine Zad. I command that the freightage of these camels be preserved in a secure place, and that any one who is afflicted by love and its passion can visit it regularly and indulge in these books that I copied from the bottom of my heart, day and night, without weakness or any passing fatigue to stop me from completing what I had intended to do one dark night among many in Damascus. Had it not been for the paralysis that first afflicted my right hand and then my left, I would have been able to live up to the promise I had made with myself before paying my debt to you, whether in your presence or in your absence, with God as my witness.

It is said that the man was buried soon after in a cemetery near the Umayyad Mosque and that his tomb had become a destination for lovers and barren women. Miracles related to him were often told, the most frequent being that a ray of light emanated from his grave the one night of the month when no moon can be seen. It is the night that the ghost of Yasmine Zad appears. As for the manuscripts that he copied by hand, they were lost in one of Tamerlane's raids on Damascus. It is said that they are stored in the library of one of the European orientalists who visited Damascus at the end of the nineteenth century, but no one knows where or even knows his name. The site of his grave has turned to dust and there is nothing left to commemorate the man called Zayd ibn Ibrahim al-Baghdadi except for a narrow alleyway in the Saruja neighborhood, but that was before the names of the streets were changed, erasing any trace of him save for one copy of Ibn Hazm al-Andalusi's famous manuscript on love, *The Ring of the Dove*, which claims that he was the first to copy it in one of the Cordoba libraries.

The idea of copying from manuscripts the most beautiful things said about love, separation, and death led me to think about al-Jahiz. I tried to remember something about him. I returned to my library, which I had not organized in at least two years, looking for some trace of this man. I will not mention at this time anything about his biography except that he died of hemiplegia in his library, his world having collapsed on him at the end of his life. When I found a book on his life and his writings, I jotted down certain lines that I thought I might need for the novel:

> I was writing a book that has many meanings and is nicely organized. I attribute it to myself even though I do not see many ears that may listen to it, nor those who may want to. Then I write what is most lacking in terms of its quality and what is least beneficial about it, and I falsely attribute this to Abdullah ibn al-Muqaffa' or Sahal ibn Harun, or one of the other predecessors whose names come up in the literary works and whose books are widely received and quickly copied.

I wrote down as well, "I had never seen or heard that he carried a book, 'He reads exhaustively, whatever it may be, even renting out scribes' shops to spend the night in them and to reflect.'"

In al-Zahiriya Library, I stood stupefied in front of shelves of old books and manuscripts. I was at a loss confronted by thousands of pages that needed to be carefully examined in search of a useful sentence or some lines of poetry. Specifically, I was looking for a book by al-Jahiz called *A Manuscript on Love and Women*, but I could not find it in the indexes as an independent work. What I did find though was a passage entitled "A Manuscript on Qiyan," which I am guessing is a section of the original work with the same title. It has a description of a qayna:

How does the qayna stay free of seduction, or, in other words, is it possible for her to be chaste? Indeed, she acquires the knowledge of passion, and at the same time learns eloquence and morals from the beginning. She is brought up from birth to the time of her death, with what prevents the invocation of God, in the pleasure of conversation and all kinds of games and mischievousness. She lives between the morally depraved and pranksters and those who never utter a serious word or resort to jurisprudence, religion, or defending the honor of manhood. The clever ones among these women will be able to recite four thousand short verses and more, this short verse being between two and four lines. A number of poems are like that, such that if ten thousand lines were mixed together, there would be no mention of God except by accident. There is neither fear of punishment nor the desire for reward. Indeed, her entirety is founded on the mention of fornication and pandering, love and passion, desire and lust. Furthermore she is constantly honing her craft; indeed she remains wholeheartedly dedicated to it. Even if she wanted to reform herself, she would not know what that was. And even if she could wish for chastity, she would not be able to attain it.

I continued visiting al-Zahiriya Library keeping in mind how great novelists construct their works: How they study and research sources relevant to the time period of the novel, to the places in which the characters exist and the temperaments that govern their behavior, the clothes they wear, even the shape of the buildings. I was on my way home, winding down streets and alleys I barely knew, thinking about their architectural construction, windows, doors, and arches. I turned down an alley in the spice quarter of the old city, taking in the aromas seeping out of the shops. I remembered the novel *Perfume* by Patrick Süskind. It cast a spell on me for some time until I came to the conclusion that it was a rather conventional novel and did not warrant the praise it had received from readers. I wished I could find a way to learn the names of all the daily household items and the seeds, grains, and herbs that crowded the storefronts. This would enrich my novel with some local flavor and imbue it with authenticity and individuality. Positioned against the curb, I noted in my journal that I needed to reread Bakhtin's *Time and Place in the Novel; The Art of the Novel* by Milan Kundera; *Obabakoak* by Bernardo Atxaga; and, of course, *How to Write a Novel*, by the beloved novelist and my dear old friend, Gabriel Garcia Marquez. Without a doubt, he is my spiritual father. I had once hoped to own his electric typewriter, the one on which he wrote his celebrated work *One Hundred Years of Solitude*, but in the last interview I read with him on the internet, I learned that he had stopped using it and had traded it in for a laptop. I have to admit

I felt sad because I still was not used to writing on a computer, only with pen and paper. Sitting on a yellow plastic chair at the kitchen table, I almost stopped writing this novel of mine when I thought about my ridiculous situation; smoking one Gitanes after another and filling the ashtray with cigarette butts like any Francophile writer anticipating the possibility that his novel will be translated into French, or that it may win the Goncourt (not altogether that difficult after Amin Maalouf won it a few years back). I also like Maalouf's work a lot. I should send him a personal note in regard to his novel *Samarkand* from which I plan to take some excerpts that are relevant to the section of my book on love and passion when I find the right narrative context.

Although I was a bit tired, I felt a feverish desire to write and decided to make myself a cup of Nescafé, the appropriate drink for someone in my condition. A writer must live the experience of insomnia as he delves into the grand entrée of the story, the secrets of the imagination, and the intrigue of creation, all the while trying to ignore screeching garbage trucks this late at night. They drove me absolutely crazy.

Needless to say, I will never be satisfied with just a few passing lines on "Gabu." This man, as I mentioned earlier, is someone I regard as a spiritual father. He taught me, in one way or another, that the novel can only be written as he had written it: that the novel's singularity, magic, and allure should completely convince you that imagination played no part, but rather it is the events themselves that weave together these cursed stories from the very first line of the novel to the last.

I read *One Hundred Years of Solitude* as soon as it came out in Arabic at the beginning of 1980. At that time, I was a miserable teacher sent by the state to a village on the edge of the desert. I had bought it with a bunch of other books during my first visit to Damascus to register for university. I consider this date to be a definitive point in my serious relationship with reading. When I think about the first book that I read, a wooden armoire on the southern wall of my grandmother's room (on my mother Fidda al-Jasim's side) immediately pops into my head. She was the first one to introduce me to the allure of narratives, like all great novelists. There in this cupboard, I would find dog-eared pamphlets scattered among all kinds of things. They were excerpts from *A Thousand and One Nights*. I remember spending long hours sprawled out on the floor of the room, reading my way into this obscure and magical world, a world not that different from my grandmother's stories of demons and seven-headed snakes that used to scare me as I fell asleep.

But Marquez led me to a much stranger world, peering into generations of a family's (whose names I found so difficult) violence, darkness, desire, naiveté, and magic. I could not, though, glean the threads of this story with my first reading. This is the complete opposite of what happened with Dostoevsky's great novel *Crime and Punishment*, one that prevented me from eating, but whose lines I devoured while sitting in the doorway of my room in that distant village while I prayed for a late sunset so that I could finish another chapter before I would need a gas lamp to read in the shadow of its muted light. Consequently, I could avoid my mother's protests that I will lose my eyesight to books, as well.

When I reread *One Hundred Years of Solitude* about ten years later, I fell in love with it in an indescribable way. I figured out without much difficulty why I loved this amazing novelist and his fantastic village, Macondo, with its gypsies, outsiders, and secrets, its fate predestined for oblivion. It occurred to me out of nowhere that Macondo was not much different from my village in its infinite solitude. But what appeared to be lacking was a dazzling character like the Colonel, or Aureliano Buendia. Throughout my life, I cannot recall anyone passing through this village or treading on its land with a rank any higher than first assistant to the commanding officer. Once in a while police troops would arrive in the village and stir up the stagnant wind of the mayor's courtyard. They would come to notify young men who had recently become old enough for military service. This would get the mothers wailing, for whoever goes returns only in a coffin, thanks to a certain hopeless war in a distant land, called "the front," which is hard to clearly imagine. How often the men would listen fearfully to this name on the one and only radio, which, by the way, my uncle owned and had bought one distant summer for the equivalent of two sheep. Everyone thought that he was absolutely crazy when he brought this devilish box home. It turned my grandmother into Sherida from the Marquez masterpiece, though I could have said Ursula as well. She would call out to God during her mysterious prayers to protect the house from evil spirits. She placed amulets in the corners of the house, as recommended to her by one of the holy saints known for blessings and miracles. As for the beautiful Remedios, I would not find anyone better than Thuraya to fill her role. I had returned home one hot summer from Damascus after finishing my exams. There was nothing to do but read, take long afternoon naps, and go out to the cotton fields at dusk to sit for hours on the banks of the river. Sometimes I would swim. Suddenly I noticed this beautiful brown-skinned girl in the sheep corral neighboring my family's house. I found out that she was the daughter of the fellah whom my father had brought from a distant village in the north to tend to the vegetables and other plants. These were people who were known for their agricultural skills and ability to profit from the land, quite unlike my 'eloquent' relations who found themselves to be proprietors of land, but were unable to reap any financial benefits from it. The fellahin harbored a nostalgia for the nocturnal desert and herding, and would sigh profoundly when thinking back to that ephemeral, happy time.

Thuraya was seventeen. She had long, coal-black curly hair, wide eyes, dimples in her cheeks, and round ample breasts. Without a doubt I knew that she was Remedios and that I had to get to know her right away before she flew off in one of the bed sheets that I imagined her in. Thuraya was in and out of the mud-brick hut that stood next to the sheep corral that had been put together and cleaned up for her family. Sometimes I would hear her voice when she was arguing with her mother, refusing to light the oven or prepare fresh-baked bread for her father, who was busy priming seeds (like tomato, pepper, and eggplant) in the courtyard. He never once raised his voice despite all the yelling going on around him. Meanwhile, Thuraya/Remedios would sit on a wooden box, not troubled at all by her mother's plea to get rid of this girl who never listened to a word and knew no shame. She carried around a small mirror in one hand, while the other would dip an applicator into kohl, applying it to her eyes with great resolve.

From the low window of my room, I would constantly think about Remedios. Suddenly, she got up and headed in the direction of our house. My heart raced out of control as she passed in front me like a storm, betraying her small white teeth and sharp arcadian scent. I felt weak.

At sunset, I noticed her once again as she was crossing the courtyard heading back toward her place. I was practically shaking when I found her in front of me. She had made her way through the house and walked right into my room by way of the open door, upon which she told me that she had been waiting for my return from Damascus after having heard about me from my sister. She then added that she had been in love with me even before ever laying eyes on me. I did not say a word. I was even more embarrassed when I noticed her looking around, especially at the door. I had a hard time getting up because I was stretched out on a felt rug and leaning against a wool pillow. I was reading one of the books I had brought back with me from Damascus. I stood up and offered her my place. She excused herself and said that she would see me soon. She left laughing, another gale of her scent trailing behind her. I felt a feverish shiver run down my spine.

The next day I decided to reopen the family store. It had been closed for months because my father was too busy with the farm and always traveling. I asked my mother, who welcomed the idea, for the key and headed toward the store, which was right next to Remedios's home. When I opened the door I was surprised by the chaos and dust, the bags of sugar, tea, and soap piled one on top of another. I started to arrange the dusty shelves. I put things in corners accordingly: perfumes, combs, kohl, and mirrors in one; hard candies, chewing gum, and pumpkin and watermelon seeds in another. Then I set the cloth and bands of silk on a shelf and soap and oils on another. I kept doing this until the place looked somewhat acceptable. I sat on one of the cane chairs behind a low ramshackle wooden table. There was a small iron scale with a locked drawer on it. This was where the money was kept. I opened it but it was empty. My father must have taken it all before setting out on his travels to the city and the outskirts to check on the unirrigated crops bordering the desert. Anyway, it was rare for one of his customers to pay with money up front. This meant that I would have to register the sales in the thick notebook on top of the table. My father had organized the pages according to the customers' residential sequence. In any event, they lived in the village and would not pay their debts until after cotton season or the wheat harvest.

As you might expect, while I was in the throes of distraction, in walked Remedios like a storm. At first, she glanced at the shelves disinterestedly and then came toward me. She lifted the wooden barrier separating the shelves from the rest of the store, where customers would sit on a clay bench that was now covered in plaster chips. Without my having moved, I found her standing next to me, her long dress grazing my trembling thighs. She grabbed a small bottle of perfume and opened it to smell what was inside. With a tinge of regret she asked how much it was. Impetuously, I told her it was a present for her. That made her quite happy. I found the courage to take her hand and without a word I led her to a corner behind the door piled high with bags of rice and sugar. I leaned over her, supporting myself on one of the bags and put my lips on hers aggressively. She protested with all her might, afraid someone might come in, but I did not get off her until my pants were soaked from succumbing to a wondrous sensation I had never felt before.

Throughout this summer, Remedios and I would meet up for some playful love occasionally. She certainly thought that this stormy romance would lead to a happy ending, and so, did not object to lying down with me among the yellow cornstalks in the afternoon, in the cows' pen, behind the courtyard of the house, between spools of cotton, or even in my room at night. Serenely she would slip in after my family had put out the lights, stretching beside me in my bed. I would explore the contours of her body and her dense labyrinth of silky reeds, her small, hard breasts, and her tender ass that had come to know my infinite desire for her. No one could hear her moans in the absolute silence of night except for me.

Remedios's attachment for me had grown to the point that our secret relationship would have surely been exposed had it not been for a burly fellah who saw her in the fields one day. She was leaning over, picking fruit from a tomato plant, when she sensed footsteps. She looked up and saw a large man leering at her. According to what she told me that same night, he immediately decided to ask for her hand in marriage. Her father agreed unconditionally and her mother blessed the affair. Afraid of an impending scandal, she felt she had found a cure for her insolent daughter's outbursts in this intrepid man. When she saw my tepid response and the weakness of my position, she buried her head in my chest and burst into tears, wailing loudly. I tried to calm her down, afraid we would be discovered. Suddenly some nearby dogs started to bark and we could hear muffled voices crossing the path opposite the open window to my room. When the voices and the barking receded, she lifted her head and peered earnestly into my eyes through the darkness. Then she began to ravage my lips, gliding her hand down my stomach to stroke that mysterious object she had all along been afraid to approach. She started to play with me, stripping me of the power to maintain my command and not caring one bit what would happen to her. She whispered in my ear that she would cleverly convince that behemoth of a man that he was the first to enter her garden, the first to pick her forbidden fruit, and the first to stroke her sublime pomegranate. I began to cave in the face of her insolence and savagery and the bed was soon soaked amid her hot moans.

That was the last time the beautiful Remedios and I were together. She left the village a few days later in the company of her groom and on the back of a donkey for a neighboring village. She appeared to be moving away, as if flying on the blankets being carried by another donkey. The village had lost its serenity after a sudden sandstorm whirled through, leaving me with a duplicitous sense of unrest and a desperate desire to leave. As Marquez had done, I tried to find my own particular solution to the enigma of whether to continue or tear up this so-called novel. But my conviction was strengthened when he confided in me, whispering, "Writing a novel is, more than anything else, building with bricks. One can always go back to it anew." In this way I started repeating, nibbling on a mealy apple, "Damn, how do you write a novel?"

I had to find that precious text, *The Ring of the Dove*, by Ibn Hazm. It seemed that my copy was abridged. So I spent the evening among the shelves of al-Zahiriya Library searching for this treasure, flagrantly embodying the spirit of Umberto Eco's *The Name of the Rose* as Eco searches for an obscure manuscript in the library of an old monastery in Italy. In the midst of my feverish search for the manuscript, which I had not hoped to find too easily, I caught sight of it on the second shelf on the southern face of the hall. I went to it quickly and was frustrated when I found it to be in good shape, as if it had been recently printed. I took it in my hands and chose a remote corner of the library. I started flipping through its pages acting as though I had not read it, at the very least, three times over the course of some years. This time what struck me was the introduction

Ibn Hazm had written for it. I felt like it could be the key to my novel. I imagined myself at one of the arcades of the castles of Cordoba strolling between pomegranate trees, repeating to myself a qasida I had written on desire in love, or on gesturing with one's eyes. If it had not been for the guffaw of the library curator on the telephone, I would still be daydreaming. I went back to the first page of the text, seduced by my literary ancestors' style in penning introductions to their manuscripts. Oh, to begin my novel this way:

> You have entrusted me, may God exalt you, to compose for you a treatise on the attributes of love, its meaning, its causes, and its symptoms, and what happens in it and to it, by way of truth and without exaggeration or bewitchment, but rather presenting what happens to me exactly and commensurate with its occurrence. And as you have charged me, I am obliged to mention what I have personally witnessed, what I have come to understand from my depths, and what has been communicated to me by trustworthy contemporaries. Please excuse the nicknames I use; this is due to either a shame I do not wish to uncover or that by this we are protecting a beloved friend and notable man.
>
> I am committed in this book to stand by your bounds, limiting myself to what I have seen or to what I know is true by transmission from those

whom I trust. Spare me from the tales of Bedouin or our literary predecessors; their way is not our way and there are more than they. It is not my practice to exhaust another's riding animal nor to adorn myself with borrowed pieces. God is forgiving and merciful. There is no God but He.

When I finished copying the introduction down, I jotted down some phrases and expressions that caught my eye on another page: "[On] Love, may God exalt you, the first part is jest and the last serious. Its meanings, in all their majesty, are too subtle to describe. Their truth can only be perceived through experience. It is neither disapproved of by religion nor forbidden by law. For hearts are in the hand of God, the mighty and sublime." Then I underlined it while looking out of the corner of my eye at a young woman who was sitting across from me and had been coming to the library the past few weeks. When she raised her eyes from the book in her hands, she noticed that I was watching her. I smiled at her, nudging a piece of paper toward her, taking courage from Abu Muhammad ibn Ahmad ibn Said ibn Hazm al-Andalusi. As soon as she finished reading it, her face paled and she threw the paper at me. I felt the need to leave immediately. When I made my way out of the lobby, I quickened my pace toward the exit door inhaling the odor of frustration that lingered in the maze of the ancient corridors. A light rain was falling on the streets. I almost yelled out, "Kiss me, Biji."

I stayed away from al-Zahiriya Library for two weeks, busying myself with organizing my own chaotic library. I found the courage to make some unequivocal decisions regarding all the trivial books in my library, especially those laden with exalting dedications: "To the one whose transparent pen never negotiates"; "With all my profound love"; or "I hope to read your opinion on this book."

At one time, that is to say about ten years ago, I hosted a radio show called *Recently Published* on Voice of the People, a station hardly anyone listened to. I also wrote literary reviews in local newspapers, which is why my library teems with these miserable books that have infiltrated my shelves in such large numbers like a colony of rats in an empty house. What was driving me crazy was that I would find some of these aforementioned books sandwiched between *Don Quixote* and *Remembrance of Things Past*, or the works of Chekhov and *Gilgamesh*. In a flagrant act, I grabbed a booklet by a poet who worked in the Department of Technical Services in one of the districts and threw it down on the ground. It was the first victim in a pile of what ended up being no less than one hundred and fifty corpses. To add insult to injury, I decided to give them to my neighbor who irons clothes for a living and is also a local musician, although he clearly stutters. I did not even consider selling them to the street vendors, as some of you will suggest. And this is for a very simple reason: these guys immediately make excuses about selling merchandise like this, claiming a profound knowledge of these kinds of books and their true value for readers. Likewise, they get rid of them immediately and bury them in a place where no hands will ever pass over them. Another convincing reason is related to a true story that happened to me a few years ago. I had decided to purge my library of anything that was defective, water-stained, or moldy, as I was doing now. I brought up one of the street vendors to my house and showed him the books I had decided to get rid of, after being satisfied that I would no longer benefit from these textual acquisitions, no matter their importance, and being sure that I would never need them again, for when would I ever need *The Letters of Rosa Luxemburg*, *Selections from Lenin*, *This is the Way We Poured the Steel*, or the novels of Ihsan Abd al-Quddous, the poetry of Nazim Hikmet, or editions of the literary journal *al-Mawqif al-adabi*, in addition to vast quantities of Arabic, Bulgarian, and Soviet poetry, novels, and philosophical and historical studies, and ones on sociology and literary heritage. The vendor recommended ripping out the dedication page and promised me, with a gentleman's agreement, that he would do just that, only charging me a small fee. Needless to say, he did not stand by his promise and on the first Friday after our agreement, he set them down on the sidewalk just as they were when they left the house, dedications and all. This caused me a great many problems. Writers chided me for what they considered to be an ignominious act on my part. One of them had written the following dedication to me: "To the kind Bedouin in cities of dust." But that 'kind Bedouin' had just sold the book for only ten liras.

After about two hours of this contentious battle, I had scores of books and papers (jammed between the shelves) piled high on the ground. The papers were nothing more than friends' addresses, newspaper clippings, electricity bills, and postcards. At the same time, I discovered a number of books I thought I had lost or no longer had, because my library was often a source for looting and theft by my friends, despite the cautious, defensive measures I took to protect those souls imprisoned between book jackets. One such secret measure was my creation of a special signet of a man with open arms that I stamped in each new book on page thirteen precisely. So, whenever I would visit a friend whom I suspected of theft, I would stand inconspicuously in front of their library while he or she was off making tea in the kitchen and start flipping through books I thought might be mine, stopping on page thirteen. Most of the time I was not disappointed.

I set aside the books I would need to construct my novel, deciding not to put them back on the shelves. It was more than I probably needed, but confidence had found its way back to my soul (the one so interested in writing a novel), and the bricks necessary for the novel's structure had started to crystallize in my mind. I resolved to divide the novel into three parts—love, separation, death—in keeping with Yasmine Zad's request to the Baghdadi trader I had conjured up at the Nawfara Café.

With that I had become totally absorbed with writing down notes related to the section on love side-by-side with my notes on how to write the novel, but now was a bit confused between all the narrative techniques: Marquez's advice; Italo Calvino's recommendations; the madness of Milan Kundera; Borges's ravings; the seductiveness of *A Thousand and One Nights*; Balzac's realism; the naturalism of Emile Zola; al-Hamadhani's maqamat. All this scatter made my head spin. I was fed up with academic work, drawing sharp distinctions between writing and life itself. I recorded the observations that I had collected up until now, just as I found them and in the same order. There was a wonderful alchemy in my narrative laboratory. Sainte-Beuve (do you know him?) said, "The novel is an expansive field among writings that takes on a demeanor able to open up all kinds of genius, as well as intrinsic qualities. It is the epic of the future." On the other hand, Marquez finds writing the novel to be a kind of puzzle of the world and a secret code where unexpected things happen while writing, because reality is not limited to the price of tomatoes or eggs, as Europeans think.

Kundera condensed the novel to a profound construct: the biography of the forgotten person. Perhaps this is what I need, "A search for what turns within," or "Discovering the secret life of emotions." He is not content with rhetoric, but rather, dives vengefully into thousands of pages written by novelists on war, among them Tolstoy. I do not remember any of his novels except for the betrayal of the noble Anna Karenina. This is what Kundera has to say: "War, at the hands of Homer and Tolstoy, has a very clear intention. The people fought for the sake of the beautiful Helen or for the sake of Russia. At that time Schweik and his compatriots headed to the front without knowing why, and without any interest in it, and this is what shocks us the most." That is exactly what I am looking for, but at the same time, I despise historical novels set during the Ottoman Empire or French colonialism or the like.

To be quite frank, I am writing this novel for the sake of the beautiful Helen, though she is not merely one person. Actually, every time I say this is my last Helen, another Helen and another and another generates. I am not a warrior in Sparta or a soldier in Safr Barlik rebelling against the Ottomans, or in Chechnya or Afghanistan, or in Bosnia and Herzegovina. I hate war. I cannot imagine myself at any time cocking a rifle to kill someone even if he were my enemy, plunging my sword in their guts, or cutting off a nose in the name of Islam, such as what is depicted in those historical

TV dramas. I do not need my name to be held in regard like Akrama, Dawqala, or Nuhaysh or some other pre-Islamic name. I only want to live in peace and to write this novel with a bit of joy and love. As James Joyce defines a novelist, "A neutral god cleaning his nails in silence." Or like the definition of the root for the word 'novelist'—*ray-waw-ya*—in *Lisan al-Arab*, quite simply, 'the flow of water.'

Yet, this is what I need: a novel that flows like a river, calm when level and fast when falling. A novel without banks, filled with fish, whales, fairies, snakes, and jinn. A novel like all sixteenth-century narratives, when Shakespeare wrote *Romeo and Juliet*, and like Antonio Skarmeta, the author whose novel inspired the film *Il Postino*. From Abu Uthman al-Jahiz ibn Bahr and Abu Hayyan al-Tawhidi to the most recent Arabic novel (author unknown) banned by the censors because of some phrases that "disturb general decency," or take on taboos. It is utterly amazing in this day and age that a few phrases or expressions can upset the inner core of al-Azhar sheikhs and their legal judiciaries, and can provoke them to impose restrictions on their writers or even call for their blood to be shed. Whereas, in the days of their forebears, words such as these were considered part of 'the sciences' in the realm of speech and opinion, and as such were included in their nightly discussions, never amounting to anything more. Who dares today to publish the wine poems of Abu Nuwas, the risqué poetry that al-Jahiz quoted in *Advantages and Disadvantages*, the original manuscript of "The Bride's Gift" by al-Tijani, "The Culture of Mumps" by Imam al-Ghazali, or *The Perfumed Garden* by al-Nafzawi. During my feverish search for texts on passion in the Arabic literary tradition—and there are hundreds—I sensed that life has been turned upside down. What we today call taboo and will not speak of at all, especially in regard to sex, was mere child's play. Following in the footsteps of these texts alone would suffice to put together an erotic novel that is as provocative, if not more so, than any book on the market today; like the British chef Gordon Ramsay's book on cooking and *Memory in the Flesh* by the Algerian Ahlam Mosteghanemi. I would give it the same name that Abu al-Hasan Ali bin Muhammad al-Dailami chose, with its sensitivity and acumen, centuries ago, *The Tenderness of the Conventional Alif for the Conjoined Lam*. Although, for it to be distinctly the readers' novel, in their capacity as participant or partner, they cannot merely be recipients because these references would become part of their memory. And while strolling through this topiary the reader would have to exert some effort to recover what happened during events, and as well to grant those people whom they already know so well some part of their imagination. Quite simply, by way of fantasy and kindling memory, the reader would be able to materialize the spirit of Aphrodite in the body of the woman who lives in the building next door, even if she's only someone who works the floor at a chocolate factory or in a sweatshop making clothes. The reader could give her Demi Moore's body from the movie *Indecent Proposal* and take advantage of her after promising to marry her, once "things get better." The reader could do that in a building vestibule under construction (after bribing the guard, of course), or at a movie theater, or any inconspicuous place. These suggestions are not merely hypothetical, they are a concrete truth that can cure innumerable ailments. Take soldiers, for instance, especially those on night duty. They think about their long-distance girlfriends all the time, much more than they think about a surprise attack by the enemy or making sure of their Kalashnikovs' range. The first thing they do when they settle into their assigned rooms is to tape posters of actresses and models over their beds (definitely not images of historical leaders and generals). While they adjust to this stark new life, these 'ladies' are merciless companions under their blankets, so much so, that they forget the password that was entrusted to them for night duty. They become totally absorbed in their fantasies, each summoning the spirit of Layla Elwi, Marilyn Monroe, or Soad Hosni on their own, and absolutely prepared to surrender every last munition and secret map in his possession, for she (whoever she is) has become that desired nation and object of self-sacrifice. Even when he finds himself in the trenches face to face with enemy tanks and bombs a few inches away, he trembles not because he is afraid of death, or of being captured and tortured for secret military information that some might venture to think he knows. No, he is terrified he may never see his girlfriend again. This is hell itself. Let us not forget that during the Vietnam War and before that in Germany, the Americans flew prostitutes to the front lines in order to help quench the fires burning inside the soldiers and to help rekindle their courage to face the enemy once again.

Likewise, the reader has to visualize his own particular fantasy and sustain the spirit in these feminine bodies that have been created by their authors in a particular way, like any intertextual state, just like what takes place in the novel that I intend to write. At this moment, there are piles of books on my table that I picked out from the shelves and read at different times and under different psychological circumstances that I now do not remember. And I do not even know exactly why I enjoyed this novel with such fervor at one time and did not finish some other novel at another. Why was I at one time interested in the works of Freud and Wilhelm Reich, in Yusuf Idris's short stories and Pushkin's poetry?

In order for me to solve this dilemma simply I would have to acknowledge that life is a story that has no end. A person's spirit takes shape slowly. Beyond any story, whether true or imagined, lurks some kind of a secret: a ring or a lamp will recede into the dream as soon as we pick one up. When discussing the narrative magic of *A Thousand and One Nights,* Borges says, "Stories within stories create a strange effect, almost infinite, a sort of vertigo. This has been imitated by writers ever since. . . . To erect the palace of *A Thousand and One Nights* it took generations of people, and these people are our benefactors, as we have inherited this inexhaustible book. . . . The infinite time of *A Thousand and One Nights* continues its course. . . ."

On the basis of this idea of syngenesis, I believe that when Faulkner wrote *The Sound and the Fury*, he was not thinking about dethroning Balzac and his ilk, or that Marquez, who revered Faulkner to the point of worship, did not think, as well, about creating magical realism as an antidote for fledgling novelists. Words have hidden secrets that can move sleeping hearts or turn them into sand. I wrote down Isabel Allende's short story "Two Words," in the hope of getting something out of it later. In it, the wonderfully named Belisa Crepusculario, who makes her living by selling words, including secret ones to ward off melancholy, is asked by the feared Colonel to write his election speech. She does so, yet although his popularity grows, the two secret words included in the price eat away at him from inside, taming his savage soul.

I now know more than at any time in the past and without a doubt that words can calm the savage beast, but only in the most extreme cases. And I now know that when asked to "give a useful sentence constructed from a subject and predicate, or a verb, subject, and object," during grammar lessons in elementary school, it was not a punitive exercise or due to the idiocy of cruel teachers, but rather, the sentences were capsules of meaning, exercises for the imagination to create useful sentences. The novels that stay with us like dreams are inevitably useful sentences that unknown friends have written for us, to help us, to make us happy, and to lighten the load of life that has turned most people into sheep and cattle running after food or committing crimes in the name of law and justice. If government agents, the police, and the miserable secret police read novels, then they would not be so crude and vacuous. This is why Shahrayar, who took the virginity of a new girl each night and then killed her in the morning, could not manage (as was his habit) to get rid of Shahrazad and the litany of stories she concocted that eventually compelled him to put off killing this grand dame until the next day, and perhaps for ever, after which a long line of storytellers and narrators followed behind her in every different corner of the world. Gabriel Garcia Marquez, one of her most famous grandsons, borrowed some of her narrative particularities, as did Isabel Allende, the writer of the story I just mentioned, and scores of unknown grandmothers, practiced bedtime storytellers like Shahrazad, who, however, are not anointed with fame.

Even Marquez himself admits, "Half of the stories that I have started to formulate, I heard from my mother. She is now eighty-seven years old and has never heard one word related to literary discourse or narrative technique or anything like that. Yet she knows how to create dramatic effect, hiding the ace in the palm of her hand with greater skill than any amateur who pulls a scarf or rabbit out of a hat." He also says in "The Blessed Whim of Narration," "I am convinced that the world is divided between those who know how to tell a story and those who do not. Just as, on a larger scale, those who shit well and those who do not." This is exactly what I want to do: to create a dramatic effect. But, "How to tell a story?" "How to completely observe the details of the imagination's whimsical comings and goings and to suddenly grasp the precise moment when an idea emerges like a hunter who all of a sudden detects the exact moment a rabbit hops into his cross-hairs?"

Finding myself in the depths of novelistic solitude, I called one of my friends, Lumia. She suggested that we go out together. Of course, I agreed immediately as romantic notions started to simmer in my mind. Although the three thousand kilometers we had covered walking Damascus streets over the past few months never led anywhere, the perfect afternoon rendezvous with her was imminent.

I got dressed immediately and left my papers on the table as they were. Within a few minutes, I was standing on the curb at Seven Spices Square waiting for her like any wanton suitor. I stretched out my hand to greet her as she approached and we started our usual aimless walk at once. She told me she was feeling bored and dissatisfied, and was thinking about leaving. I replied like any wise Hindu calmly, "What you lack is love; you feel a romantic void. I vow to take care of this matter." She looked at me scornfully and hit me on the shoulder. I thought this was a fortuitous opportunity to take her arm in mine, but she withdrew her hand quickly.

"Are you crazy?" she said.

"Crazy in love with you."

We headed in the direction of Victoria Square, then toward al-Hijaz Street. Passing across from the Hijaz Train Station, I suggested that we go in and have a coffee at the café. In the interior courtyard of the station, the Railway Administration had cleverly converted one of the train cars into a café. It was the same car that the Ottoman sultan Abd al-Hamid had stood upon to inaugurate the first pilgrim voyage from Damascus to Mecca, the illuminated city, on August 22, 1907. The journey would have taken roughly fifty-five hours. There we sat across from each other in that very compartment, sipping coffee far from the other tables scattered around the car. I was thinking about making a pilgrimage to her house soon and so stretched my hand out and placed it on her fingers. I imagined that she was as taken with the splendor of the place as I, and enchanted by my knowledge of the history of the station, which was designed, more than a hundred years ago, by the Spanish architect Fernando de Aranda with careful attention to the aesthetics of Islamic architecture. As the biggest train station in the Ottoman Empire at the time, it was considered a unique architectural gem. But in all honesty, she was distracted and had only come out to pass some time. "Let's go," she blurted suddenly. We spent most of the next two hours wandering the streets, from the citadel to the sidewalks alongside the Umayyad mosque that lead to al-Qamariya neighborhood, Bab Tuma Square, and finally to the vicinity of al-Abassiyyin, where she lives. I found the courage to steal a kiss at the entrance to her building and then caught a taxi to my house feeling an uncanny sense of levity. Not because of the kiss—that had already happened a few times—but rather because of an acute sensation that I had finally found the key to my novel. All the previous keys that I had tried were thwarted by rusty locks and faulty doors. And when they did open, I could not make it through the narrow hallways to the house that I wanted to furnish with the souls of my characters and their impending fates.

This did not bother me too much. I was still in the early stages of this folly. I took refuge in what Gaston Bachelard said in *The Poetics of Space*: "In the realm of ideas, there is not a principal or initial truth, but rather, a maneuvering from revision to revision as we try to arrive at a sound idea. There are only initial mistakes. The scientific concept has a long history of initial mistakes, whereas the imaginative one has none. Its poetics, that is the word's moment, is incompatible and contradictory to all that precedes it." This is exactly what was happening to me. Nothing more than a sentence of initial mistakes. And because I am a man of imagination and not science, I think that everything that affects my creative vision might lead me to a sound idea in the formation of this so-called novel of mine.

In the taxi, the initial images that began to materialize in my mind were of the Hijaz Railway Station. This place had piqued my interest every time I passed it. But today, after descending the few steps of Sultan Abd al-Hamid's carriage with Lumia, I was suddenly overcome with a sensation that, without exerting much effort, I was holding a falcon. I decided to begin the novel with what happens between a young man from Damascus and a pretty young Turkish woman as they leave Istanbul in one of the earliest train journeys from Damascus to Haifa about a hundred years ago. She is on her way to meet her husband who has recently been appointed a secretary in the governor of Jerusalem's office. They sit together in the same compartment. Rather than talking about the miracle of traveling so fast by train, they spend almost thirty-six hours in such a state of exhilaration that the young man is left in tatters, descending the wharf of Haifa's port like a sleepwalker.

I was mesmerized by this idea for the two hours I spent with Lumia in the streets. I made some pretty strong passes at her. For instance, I had said to her, "What if I were to pull down the blinds of the car and the train started to move miraculously. I think fifty-five hours would be enough time for me to crush your ribs." Despite her protests against the idea, she played along with the game. In a narrow alleyway, about a yard wide, she suddenly turned toward me and said resolutely, "I'm the one who's going to crush your ribs, not you. I have enough experience to fuel a train to the Red Sea." I squeezed her hand hard and pulled her behind me until we reached the dark end of the narrow corridor. I retorted, "What if I threw you down here?" But she slipped out of my hands, cleaning the dirt off her coat. She straightened her dress without worrying about the looks of passersby.

Of course, I did not tell her about my plan to write a novel. She does not know anything about my literary interests outside my job as a librarian at the Ministry of Education library, and some articles and bygone stories I had published in local newspapers. I met her a year ago at least, when she came to borrow the novel *Memory in the Flesh* by Ahlam Mosteghanemi after having heard a lot about it. Unsurprisingly, the book was not in the library, so I told her, "I will bring you a copy from my personal library." We agreed to meet again. As she was leaving, I could not help noticing her lovely behind stuffed into a pair of tight jeans. Before reaching the door, I said to her, "What do you think about us meeting this evening and I'll bring you the novel then?" She thought about it for a minute, then nodded. We agreed to meet at al-Riwaq Club. I was almost flying with wings of desire. After getting myself into this mess with a promise, I set out for al-Nobel Bookstore to buy a copy of the novel about an hour before our appointed meeting time. I actually had not read it yet. I felt an aversion to this novel that had become the talk of literary circles and society ladies and housewives.

The copy I bought was stamped "tenth printing." From there, I set out for my rendezvous on foot. I cut across al-Hamra Street in order to feed my imagination with tantalizing images of colliding bodies, as on the Day of Resurrection. Then I headed toward Arnous Plaza, on through al-Talyani neighborhood, and finally to al-Afif where our meeting was to be.

Lumia had previously been a teacher. She taught Women's Art before transferring to the ministry as an executive secretary in the Department of Theater for Schools. I had noticed her in the hallways occasionally but dismissed getting to know her because I sensed her intractability—that she was a recalcitrant lioness. I had heard many stories about her, one being that she did not take pleasure in other people's ideas. Yet, she certainly took pleasure in mine. But what is standing in the way of my becoming one of her victims? It is important that the right moment arrives so that she turns her attention to me. I need to get close to her. And here is the moment approaching on two feet.

I had arrived about seven minutes early for our date. I chose a remote table and started to flip through the book, looking for a sentence to use in the dedication I wanted to write. At any rate, it is merely a code for seduction. I sought inspiration in the word 'flesh' for a caption that could embody all the messages I had put off sending her. Then I lit one of my hand-rolled cigarettes and exhaled the smoke high into the air with a sense of pride. When she appeared in the doorway, my heart beat in a way it never had before. I almost did not recognize her with her sexy hairdo and cleavage partly exposed. She stood for a moment searching for me with her eyes. I waved from my remote corner. I was much more of a mess than I expected. All the plans that I had mentally prepared before her arrival had quickly disintegrated, but the first glass of beer helped me regain my balance. I thought our first meeting had gone well, especially since she asked me to accompany her to Arnous Plaza before taking a taxi home.

After we left, she asked me unexpectedly, "What will you do while I'm gone?"

I answered her immediately, "Think about you."

She laughed cheerfully, "I don't believe you."

I said, grabbing her hand, "Time will reveal that to you." A feeble attempt at philosophizing by quoting a line from the poem "The Stranger's Bed" by Mahmoud Darwish before we reached the Plaza. She hailed a taxi suddenly.

I turned to her, "What happened?"

"I have a headache. Maybe it's from the beer."

Then she opened the door and got in. I closed the door behind her, dragging my tail in defeat as if I were just leaving the shade of al-Manfaluti's linden tree.

I strolled through the streets before returning home and descending, for the thousandth time, the nine steps to my dark basement. When I opened the door, I headed straight for the bathroom to relieve myself. I replayed the failed scenario that I had worked out to seduce her with, one that was supposed to have led her by the nose here to my home so that she could pick out any novel she wanted. Meanwhile only one notion came to mind: that together we would write a novel that had never been written, on sheets embroidered with roses.

In order to get over my frustration, I turned my attention once again to the fate of my novel and the train station, being convinced of its viability even though I did not have the time to loll about writing description like Emile Zola, Balzac, or Tolstoy. All I would need is half a page on the history of the station, and perhaps on the rituals of the pilgrimage procession before the advent of this colossal iron machine. Anyway, what is the use of describing a coal-powered train in the age of electric ones?

However, an article I read in an illustrated magazine on the history of the Hijaz Railway provoked me to write down some crucial details: Damascus used to be a center of departure to holy sites; the hajj procession (made up of people from all parts of the Islamic world) would assemble here to begin a long harsh journey of fifty days there and fifty days back, not to mention the risks encountered on the caravan route: floods and torrents in the winter and the burning sun in the summer, as well as the dangers of certain parts of the route. It was the responsibility of the governor of Damascus, who would appoint a general on behalf of the Ottoman sultan, to assure the safety of the procession by accompanying it throughout the more than fifteen hundred kilometers (I almost said parasang) and approximately four hundred and ninety hours of travel divided into forty legs; ten thousand soldiers, on foot, horse, and camel, guarded the procession, which, according to historical sources, could be as long as four kilometers in some seasons.

The idea of constructing a railway to connect the Arab states goes back to the year 1864, at the time of the work on the Suez Canal, when an American engineer of German descent, Dr. Zamil, suggested the extension of a railway connecting Damascus to the Red Sea. The Sublime Porte in Istanbul did not support the idea until 1900, when, in the middle of April of that year, Sultan Abd al-Hamid announced the plan for the Hijaz Railway, considering it to be a philanthropic and religious act.

He initiated the donations himself, recording the first amount for the project's coffer to be valued at three hundred and twenty thousand gold lira. The Shah of Iran contributed fifty thousand gold lira, while the Egyptian khedive contributed huge quantities of timber and building materials. Over a number of months, eight and a half million gold lira was collected, more than enough to begin work on the project immediately. Construction continued for seven years, through harsh and difficult conditions. It concluded in an official opening on July 1, 1908, which coincided with the installment of Sultan Abd al-Hamid II on the Ottoman throne. In attendance were thirty thousand invitees and no small number of foreign journalists to cover this momentous event. A year later, Sultan Abd al-Hamid II was deposed, and the outbreak of the First World War soon followed. The Ottomans used the railway to transport their troops to the Arabian Peninsula. This was the time of the Great Arab Revolt for the Arabs to rid themselves of Ottoman occupation and in which Lawrence of Arabia found a favorable opportunity to destroy the railway on behalf of the British.

The famous English colonel's objective was not purely military; rather, he wanted to sever communication completely between Greater Syria and the Arabian Peninsula. When the First World War ended, the Arab government in Damascus took charge of repairing the railway and Prince al-Husayn ibn Ali undertook the first trip from Mecca to Damascus to visit his brother King Faysal in 1919. Subsequently, Jewish leagues in Palestine seized half of the iron bridge between al-Hama and Samakh, leading to the disruption of communication between Syria and Palestine in 1946.

After checking these details and histories, I found myself in a conundrum: How was Abd al-Rahman al-Nishwati, the name of my adventurous young man from Damascus, going to meet up with a Turkish woman after the end of Ottoman occupation in Palestine? What would a Turkish woman be doing in Jerusalem when there would no longer be a Turkish governor? What would happen to a petty administrator? Accordingly, what would Abd al-Rahman al-Nishwati be doing in this embroiled region during the First World War? And after it, the only thing to do would be to join al-Husayn ibn Ali's army or transport secret messages from Damascus. If he follows this track, then he will have to meet up with an Englishwoman, though I think it will be hard for me to convince the reader to imagine a carefree night with a frigid Brit. So, I gave up on this idea, running as far away as I could from an inevitable atmosphere of war, which I detest. All that I seek to attain is "enjoyment and conviviality," like my first literary grandfather Abu Hayyan al-Tawhidi, although I was quite certain that my aspirations were greater than any novelistic ability. Boredom is one of my favorite pastimes and my enthusiasm for completing this novel may end up in a few days to be nothing more than a sad memory, like all the love stories I have embarked on and all the careers I have worked at. When I was a university student, I worked for a time as a cultural editor at one of the wretched newspapers. I was supposed to come up with pertinent topics for a paper that was completely focused on agriculture and animal husbandry. The editor-in-chief was so pleased with my literary style that he would sometimes commission me for issues related to the countryside, checking into the situation among fellahin unions, cow farms, the estimated yields for the coming wheat season, beneficial ways to develop potato agriculture, and the tomato recession in the canning plants.

All I would end up doing was to bury myself in the archives for hours in order to 'borrow' previously published topics. I would resurrect them anew, like someone gulping castor oil, adding some spice and rhetoric, and mixing it with a hollow romanticism to describe the countryside. This is what charmed the heart of the editor-in-chief and provoked my colleagues' envy at the newspaper. Then I would disappear for a week and come back to take control of things and celebrate at the relatively inexpensive al-Qandil restaurant, where one finds the union, a not insignificant number of whose members have taken pseudonyms (both in secret and in public). Some deserve the notoriety bestowed upon them in literary circles before they were overrun by steamy headlines in the literary papers, originating from nameless editors or readers who lived on the outskirts, where they have nothing better to do than expose these types of scandals as a kind of revenge on the urban literati in the capital.

Subterfuge is not a simple operation as some amateurs believe. It is much more difficult than preparing a sample of feces in a small clean bottle, bringing it back to a lab for medical analysis, and waiting for the test results.

Bernando Atxaga, the Basque novelist, put together a complete agenda for assuming a pseudonym with five hard-and-fast rules. I think that the second one is the most useful: He who takes a pseudonym need not expend too much energy in order to reach his goal ingenuously. He must not seek out remote quarters or dark alleys, as if he were a petty thief. Instead, he should spend the middle of the day at wide open spaces in the center of the capital, heading out to Balzac Boulevard, Hardy Gardens, Hoffman Street, or Pirandello Square; in other words, he should choose his patterns from the works of writers whose names are universally well known and familiar to all. And he should not worry about that. No one will discover him because the classical writers, like the archangels, are known only by their names and icons.

In order that those without much talent do not just jump on the first novel that crosses their path, thinking of it as a blind man's cane, they should be on guard for "a stroke of bad luck," since they may easily be found out especially in an environment like ours ("filled with scheming, malice, and animosity"). It is also possible that the complete opposite may happen. The pseudonymous should, then, leave from "his adversaries' net when it has become quite hard." Without naming names, I can come up with a long list of famous novelists and poets who write under pseudonyms. They sign new material at book fairs or legal contracts for the translation of their works into other languages, certain that foreign translators are more ignorant than the proprietors of local publishing houses, given that they are so enchanted by the East and its marvels at the hands of these novels' authors or, more precisely, 'their pseudonyms.' It is not enough to take refuge in historical documents in order to fashion a novel while one's imagination sleeps under the seven layers of wet earth like a sticky bat. The best alias in the world would knock precipitously at my door. I always expected *Il Postino*'s Mario Jimenez to surprise me at any moment, forcing his presence on my imagination. Often I have put off this exceptional moment, ever since I first started preparing my novel, afraid of not granting it the reception it absolutely deserved. Neruda's personal mailman is a legendary creature without equal, created by Antonio Skarmeta's mind as a gift to me and millions of other readers. It is one of those novels you will absolutely never forget, like a stolen first kiss, the smallpox vaccination, or those distinctive tribal tattoos.

The one who enters though, slipping in through an open door, is not Mario Jimenez exactly, but Massimo Troisi, who plays the role of Mario in the film directed by Michael Radford in 1994. He is no less enchanting than in the novel with all of his paleness and the chatter of his teeth, carrying the mail bag, one of the last copies of Neruda's collections that the poet had gifted to him, and some papers that he had 'borrowed' from Neruda's poems in order to seduce the barmaid, Beatrice Gonzalez. He had been given the pseudonym 'metaphors.' In just a few seconds, I replayed the complete tape of what happens in the novel. I would love to write down one hundred and thirty-three complete pages, if I would not be accused of the largest act of literary 'borrowing' done by an unknown writer. But I can at least borrow the theme: Beatrice's mother sees the effect of Mario's metaphors on her daughter—"her smile is a butterfly fluttering on her face, her laugh a sudden silvery wave"— and warns her that the postman not only has a tongue, but also hands. She locks her away in her room. Mario begs Neruda, in the name of all his poetry about love, to talk to the mother. He does so, but is firmly rebuffed: "With those metaphors, my dear Mr. Pablo, he has made my daughter steamier than an already hot bath. And the most serious offense is that these metaphors were shamelessly taken from your work." Beatrice, however, sneaks out and gives herself to Mario, having been seduced by metaphors.

And just as in any other romantic love story, Mario ends up in the bar's kitchen cutting onions for drunken fishermen, while Beatrice (who is like a butterfly) is up to her ears tending to the fruit of their love, Pablo Nifalti, who suffers from uncountable illnesses according to the doctors treating him.

About eight years previously, Marquez had finished his famous gem, *Love in the Time of Cholera,* whose hero was also a postman, but his suffering in love was much more devastating than what Mario endured. When Florentino Ariza was returning to the telegraph center after delivering an urgent telegram, he noticed a young woman lifting her gaze to see who was passing in front of the window of her house. This fleeting gaze was "the source of a catastrophic love that did not end after a half a century." Despite the differences between the two lovers, although they both bear the makings of the simple-minded, Mario distinguished himself because he was able, with his borrowed lines of poetry, to capture the heart of his beloved after only a few months. Meanwhile, Florentino endures the pains in his chest until the moment the husband of Fermina Daza (the young woman he has silently loved) dies. After the burial rituals have ended he appears in front of this woman draped in black and mourning her lost husband to say with complete composure, "Fermina, I have waited for this opportunity for more than half a century to reiterate once again my oath of eternal loyalty and everlasting love." The miserable telegraph employee had not stopped thinking about her for a moment, ever since she had flat-out rejected him immediately after a long and troubled affair. "Fifty-one years, nine months and four days have passed since that time." Like an unexpected earthquake, he finally found himself on a riverboat traversing torrents of water fueled by wood and the love that Florentino Ariza still carried in his slender chest toward Fermina, as if the two of them were in their twenties and he could play for her his "Waltz of the Crowned Goddess" on the violin after practicing for only half a day. "And here on this boat he commands the sailboat's captain, a lifetime delayed by fifty-three years, six months and eleven days and nights."

The tropes that Marquez borrowed were taken from an actual love story between his parents, as he subsequently acknowledged in a newspaper interview. It was nothing more than a simple framework in which to construct this towering body made up of their sighs, expectations, and passionate love letters. They are the bricks that connect the structure of the novel, so that it will not fall on the heads of passersby with the first winds of a storm. This is what I told myself while diving into the maze of notes I had collected on scattered sheets of paper, written in haste, afraid of losing them. Sometimes in the darkness of sleep I would jump as if stung, groping around for the pen that I had set next to the bed to deal in particular with this kind of surprise attack.

On the edge of one of the papers I found a note in pencil: Nizar Qabbani! Immediately I remembered the situation that led me to think about Nizar Qabbani rather than someone else. During my preoccupation with the concept of pseudonyms, an ambiguous idea swirled around my head. Hundreds of lovers had shortened the distance between themselves and their beloveds' windows by stealing lines of Nizar Qabbani's poetry. It went so far as to even imagine that children of some of these exchanges would wet, during the night, the same bed that witnessed their first confections of love. Sobbing virgins would swear on their mothers' lives that the poem, "Your Body is My Map," or "Childhood Graffiti," or "Childhood Bosoms," or even "If My Beloved Were a Tree," was not just some metaphor or passionate affair behind curtains, but rather a genuine truth and anesthetic-free deleterious act in which the delicate forest of lace at the vertex of their thighs would transform into a puddle of blood in which thousands of invisible bodies swim, without . . . matrimony.

In the throes of my novelistic fury, I became convinced that I needed to reread Nizar Qabbani's poetry, although I had already read it at least a quarter of a century ago. (Meanwhile I cannot successfully recall delving into any passionate adventures.) I was content to write somber poems in my school notebook. I considered it my first poetry manuscript. I lost the manuscript before finding anyone to write to, anyone to share my passionate fire with and cure my burning love, because none of the girls I knew at that time took reading and writing seriously. They had never heard of the poet

Nizar Qabbani at all. Perhaps it was a sound judgment on my mother's part to use the papers of this sad notebook to fuel the fire and slowly boil the wheat that would turn into our meals of creamy bulgur on cold wintry nights.

I could not find even one Nizar Qabbani collection in my library. I remembered that I gifted them to someone who suffered from the curse of love postponed. There was nothing I could do to revive the spirit of this poet except by putting on a thick overcoat and heading out into the street that bears his name in the Abu Rumani neighborhood. It was named in his honor immediately after his death and has become a mecca for lovers. Standing alone in the middle of a snowy windstorm, I found inspiration after Lumia excused herself, over the phone, from accompanying me, and expressing her surprise at this type of request at such a late hour. To minimize the echo of my disappointment, she let out a coughing fit to assure me she has been stretched out in bed, accompanied by antibiotics, with a bad case of flu for two days.

I wandered back and forth on Nizar Qabbani Street for about half an hour and did not notice any lovers besides myself. I did, meanwhile, pique the interest of the military guards in front of one of the foreign embassies. A foot patrol squad planted themselves in front of me suddenly.

"Are you looking for something you lost on this street?" the leader of the patrol asked me.

I answered him, a bit confused, "No. Nothing."

"Well then, what are you doing here?"

"Nothing. I'm waiting for a taxi."

"Your identity card."

I bumbled about and took out my identity card. He examined it closely, then stared at me with an expectant look. "Taxis don't come down this street," he informed me.

I left quickly so as not to arouse any more suspicion, sneaking into the first alley I passed in order to stop their gazes (which, without daring to turn back, I knew were directed right at me) from burning a hole in me. My sweaty palms were demolishing a bunch of jasmine flowers I had picked off one of the building walls in the street.

I almost cursed the hour that I decided to include the biography of the 'poet of love' in my novel, although I did not relinquish the idea of visiting his grave soon at Bab al-Saghir Cemetery in al-Shaghur neighborhood to record what is written on his gravestone as a kind of requisite documentation. He is the first contemporary poet to be accused of apostasy. Even the imam of a London mosque refused to pray for his body before the plane landed at Damascus Airport.

That night I did not sleep well. I was struck by a sudden fear that I was being watched. I almost fainted when I heard the doorbell ring over and over again. I thought for a second that I had fallen into a trap without any friends discovering my tragic fate. I approached the door on tiptoe and peered through the peephole, my fingers trembling. The ghost of a person I could not recognize in the dim light appeared before me. It was not, for sure, Hamlet's father, nor even the ghost of Mut'ib al-Hadhal in *Cities of Salt.* My fear intensified. At that moment I was preparing my defense statement to prove my innocence from any accusation of harming state security. I finally opened the door to find myself face to face with a childhood friend who had felt a sudden desire to see me after such a long time. I felt reassured and invited him in. Then, out of the blue he blurted, "I came over to invite you to go out tonight. I have the boss's car at my disposal." I apologized, declining his offer because of all the things I was busy with. He sipped his tea and left, disappointed with the coldness of my reception. I went back to my bed as though afflicted with a fever, shaking under the thick blankets, like Raskolnikov the moment he finished killing the old pawnbroker in *Crime and Punishment.* I was in a state of regretful lamentation for my entire political history. I found it to be almost entirely clean except for one black spot that I knew would lead to my absolute ruin.

In the year 1982, after Israeli tanks rolled onto the streets of Beirut, emotions were running extremely high. As zealous university students, we had tasted for the first time, and completely untainted, the bitterness and shame of defeat. We had lived the old defeats as was necessary. This was a real defeat; it stood naked and submissive before us. Protesting was the only way to defy it, which we did both publicly and silently. And we followed the news, read newspapers, and listened to the songs of Marcel Khalife during raucous late nights that culminated in human carnage as witnessed by the smell of wine, tobacco, and sex that oozed from it. It must have been my inauspicious luck that led me to run into Sana Hasan, one of the members of our old coterie, in the middle of al-Salihiya Street four years later. I had just left an afternoon showing at the al-Kindi Theater. She hugged me with a sense of yearning, opening her arms in an expression of surprise as she bombarded me with questions about my life. She had moved to Latakia after graduating from the College of Fine Arts. I no longer knew anything about what was going on with her. I invited her to my house. She agreed on the condition that we go out together later that evening to meet up with friends we have in common and reminisce about "Andalusia of Yesteryear," as our group was called.

In bed, I was reminded of her old scent, something like cinnamon, and the specters of our raucous nights. She reminded me of details I had forgotten, or better yet, had tried to forget. Before getting up from our disorderly afternoon nap, she turned to me with a threatening look, "Why didn't you marry me at the time, you bastard?"

I didn't answer her. I was preoccupied with staring at the ceiling. She got up suddenly and dressed quickly.

"I'll make coffee, then we'll go," she said.

I nodded my head in agreement. When she got to the door of the room, she turned to me and said, "I swear that I didn't cheat on you. Najwa Mardini tried to get between us. And unfortunately, she succeeded. Anyway, she was the slut of the group."

She withdrew into the kitchen and then said in a loud voice, "I heard that she went to Sweden with an Iraqi political refugee. Middle-aged, just like her."

Then she added as if talking to herself, "Birds like her fall."

The gathering that brought us all together in a rented room in a narrow alley in the Palestinian refugee camp was anything but homogenous. I could not find myself in this place. I was silent the whole time, preoccupied with a way to get out, especially when the clapping suddenly grew louder. Someone stood up and took out an oud. Playing and singing, his voice sounded like a howl pounding mercilessly on the rhythmic meters of Mahmoud Darwish, Samih al-Qasim, and Ahmed Fouad Negm's poetry. When he started in on the first stanza of the poem, "I Yearn for My Mother's Bread," his voice was interrupted by the hammering of the doorbell. Someone quickly got up and, as soon as he opened the door, was met with a powerful slap on the face from a large man wearing a black suit. Three more like him scattered about the place. All of us ended up in the back of a Range Rover and from there to a table facing a boorish detective. Afterward each one of us filled out a form that required our names, the names of our mothers, aunts, and their husbands, and a brief outline of our lives.

Soon after, the telephone of this wide room in which we were all gathered rang. The man set down the receiver and asked wearily, "Who's the political singer?" The singer's face paled, "I am." He gestured with his finger for him to go into the neighboring room. As we were leaving that huge building at the break of dawn, "Victor Jara" told us that the detective had asked him to recite one of his political songs. He did and the detective looked at him with disgust saying, "Get out of my face. Damn you and whoever wrote your report."

I moved away quickly, then heard Sana's voice asking me to stop. I did.

"I'm sorry," she said. She kissed me and said, "I'm going."

"Where to?" I asked.

"Latakia." And she started to move away.

"Wait," I said, "I'll take you to the station."

After reviewing my drafts, which I had produced in what appeared to be a frenzy over a number of days, I rejected outright the transgressions that transpired. The fact that the first thing I noticed concerned my profession was like a slap in the face. The truth of the matter is I had never in my life worked as a librarian, nor even as a cashier in a bookstore. My relationship with the Ministry of Education does not go beyond a superficial geographical knowledge of the ministry building, through one of my friends who lives in an annex directly facing it.

Of all the annoying things that the protagonist would say (while I was hiding behind him as the narrator), what bothered me most was that it was in no way logical that the library of the ministry would hold the kinds of books that are mentioned. Of course, the majority of books in this library would be educational, historical, recent books donated by 'official' poets at national occasions, novels that encourage virtue specifically aimed at young and teenage girls, and some dictionaries and books of cultural heritage that usually arrive as part of a gilt-edged collection. I got my hands on a copy of *The Book of Songs* by Abu al-Faraj al-Isfahani a few years ago. I showcased the eleven editions on a shelf in my library with pride. I had often tried to read parts of it, but never had much luck, in particular because of the predominance of expressions like, "Someone said that someone mentioned someone else . . . ," and so on. My lungs would constrict and become short of breath. Instead of wasting my time with these preambles, I could have finished reading an entire story by Chekhov or Zakariya Tamer.

At the time, I was receiving a negligible salary from an institution for arts production. It was compensation for nominal work at a quarterly magazine entitled *The*

Silver Screen, although it was published, miraculously, once a year, and was filled with light and old fare. At a time when Meryl Streep, Sophie Marceau, and Catherine Deneuve were on the red carpet before photographers' lenses at the Cannes Film Festival, it was possible that in the latest edition of *Silver Screen* what could be read was a detailed report on the previous year's Cannes festival, under the title, "The Cannes Festival (Special Edition) in the Strangest Scoop I've Read in My Life." Because the office of the magazine was located on the ground floor of the institution's building, I would often run into directors, actors, writers, film critics, and young actresses. It was here that I first met Lumia, and not in the Ministry of Education's library as I claimed in the first draft.

She came to me, based on the recommendation of a friend, to help her land a role in one of the films still in pre-production, since the director of the film was one of my dearest friends. After seeing her in my office, I first convinced him to give her a screen test and then I convinced her to come back for another visit. The competition for the role of the heroine was narrowed down to her and Samar Sami. This led to intimate sittings that would start out with a discussion of her role in the scene and would end up with my underhanded manipulation to a whole other scenario after my tragic discovery that she had the most beautiful lips on earth and the most wonderful breasts in Syria. The path to the silver screen appeared to be paved with silk, like a pothole-free highway, except for a conspiracy that was hatched against us that brought an end to the matter. This is what I convinced her of, sadly, since I was losing an opportunity to discover a true star, and told her so humbly and in sorrow as she undid her bra, while thanking, in private, the person who thought of inventing the bicycle because it was the reason she had lost her virginity, according to what she told me in al-Latirna Restaurant during our second meeting outside of my office.

I was on the verge of cursing the moment I thought of writing a novel, as I plowed through dozens of lethal mistakes that piled up in front of me like street signs written in red to underscore their cautious nature: "No Passing," or "Pedestrians Have the Right of Way," or "Slow down, Dangerous Curve." If it had not been for the intervention of my friend, "Gabu," perhaps for the thirtieth time and at the right moment, then I would have stopped at these bounds of chatter and lies. At the eleventh line of the addendum he attached to *The General in His Labyrinth*, his expression glittered like crystal. In it he revisits the conditions surrounding the writing of this novel that required him to peruse thousands of documents as if they were a remedy for life or death, never once forsaking "the rules of the novel that break all the rules."

This is it, I said to myself happily, no less excited than Archimedes' cry when he discovered the law of gravity as he was leaving the bathroom. Yes, I had to violate the rules of the novel, to shift easily between crises and characters as if I were at my family house in the country, where a wondrous architecture, resulting from my father's ill-suited nightly improvisations, would find the guest room abutting the store room, which leads to the kitchen whose back window hangs over the sheep pen, and from there to the silo and the hay loft (stacked with straw) that adjoins my room, and finally, to the room with the fireplace which is used in the winter to prepare saj bread.

Therefore, I do not find it difficult to quote a news item published in a local paper a few months ago on the killing of a young woman from the rural region of Aleppo by a bullet from her brother because he discovered, on a recent visit to her house, that she regularly listened to the songs of Umm Kulthum when alone. He considered this sudden transformation in her personality a definite sign of the ruin of his family's honor (there's more than meets the eye), despite the distressed husband's confession to the police that it was he who brought her the Umm Kulthum tapes to keep her entertained while alone because he, meanwhile, was absent for long periods of time working as a mill day laborer in one of the workshops on the city outskirts earning three hundred pesos (sorry, three hundred Syrian lira). This is what the police officer on duty recorded in his official report of the incident's details.

This news item, published at the bottom of the "Incidents" page in just a few lines, did not provoke the kind of uproar I would have expected. For the first time in history, as far as I know, a woman is sentenced to death for listening to Umm Kulthum. A dark sensation came over me at the time; perhaps it is possible to employ this incident exactly as it stands in structuring a novel built on a base of Umm Kulthum's songs and this era. As a preliminary exercise, I collected all the tapes I had of the "Star of the East" and started listening to them anew in a feeble attempt to summon the spirit of the dead woman. In my mind I sketched out an absurd image of the situation: The moment the bullet was fired; the victim's last breath; all the while Umm Kulthum's voice goes round: "How can I forget my memories when they are the dreams of my life?"

I became obsessed. Everyday I would make frantic tours of the cassette shops and buy Umm Kulthum songs. I would read everything about her biography, even poetic books on the most famous singers that are sold on sidewalks. My new behavior provoked Lumia's skepticism as she accompanied me on these mysterious tours of cassette shops, without my explaining exactly the reason for my sudden interest in Umm Kulthum. When she insisted on knowing the reason, I replied, "I want to give an academic lecture on Umm Kulthum's musical films." She was not satisfied with that answer. Entering a shop selling old cassettes in Sha'lan, she said to me, "You know, the role of the harebrained lover doesn't suit you." I turned toward her and looked into her eyes, "Your eyes took me back to days gone by, and taught me to regret the past and its wounds."

In a nearby coffee shop, I showed her my research on the novel I wanted to write and also turn into a made-for-TV movie if a director picked up the idea. Of course, she would get the lead on the condition that she excuse herself from rehearsals for a play in which she had a small role. I convinced her that much greater opportunities lay ahead than mere secondary roles in a national theater production. And so she promised to stop playing the part and use it as an opportunity to smash the nose of the director who had been circling her like a wild bull since spring.

Of course, the film never happened because I did not finish writing the novel, basically because of a power play between myself and the director who insisted on writing the screenplay himself after reading my preliminary sketches for the idea. He wanted to turn it into a melodrama more suitable for the life of Farid al-Atrash and completely irrelevant to the background of the event from which it originates. At a poignant moment, I gave Lumia half of the tapes as a gift, so that she could get into the spirit. I also recommended that she listen carefully to the musical cadences in the song "The Servitude of Love" by al-Qasabji and the instrumental introduction by the composer Muhammad Abd al-Wahhab in the song "You are My Life."

In the hope of making a clean sweep, as they say, I went back to the piles of books I had put aside and started to sift through them once again. I set the books I considered to be on love first in line, and would focus exclusively on those concerned with separation and death, according to the schematic I had set up for my novel, later. From among a long line of ancestors who stayed up late each night to endure the hardships of composing books on love, passion, and pleasure, I felt, once again, a close connection between myself and al-Jahiz. I was quite sure we were both earth signs. He was the type who would only lift his turban for that which he could touch; in other words, he only dealt with tangibles. He would confront, courageously and quite frankly, facts and pronunciations and conspicuously drop from his dictionary what they call in the field of rhetoric, metonymy and pun. It suffices that he said, "Some who appear devout and ascetic . . . , he would cite them] . . . are . . . abhorred and dejected. Most often when we find a man like that he is not a man of knowledge, generosity, nobility, or dignity except to the extent of this affectation." Also, "Indeed, I wrote these expressions for native speakers to use them." (The ellipses are there in the text, omissions made by the editor of the book because of some kind of sexual inhibition. God knows why.)

Al-Jahiz also uses a profound expression, "artificial civility." This is what a handful of editors of classical texts and translations are doing under the auspices of "a revised and augmented edition" or "a loose conveyance." What really gets me are those footnotes that say, "I took it upon myself to remove any expressions or phrases that might violate public decency," as if this editor or translator had just been appointed a judge in Basra. It is well known that most of the writers of these books were legal scholars, and not merely linguistic virtuosos at newspapers, publishing houses, and universities.

When I finished cataloging my sources, it was, according to my clock, three minutes past one in the morning. This meant that I had spent almost five hours in my library. I got up and headed for the refrigerator to find something to eat, but the shelves were completely empty, save for a chunk of dried-out cheese. I devoured it immediately to ease the acidity that had started to drip in my stomach. In the kitchen I looked for some something to relieve my stomach. I took an antacid, and consoled myself thinking: How can writers remember to eat when they are, with complete abandon, in the grips of a decisive moment that arises from some character's affair or one that may lead them down to the depths? Certainly, the pack of cigarettes that I had smoked is not at all an issue. In his youth, Marquez would smoke forty cigarettes a day. Me, I never smoke more than thirty. I had hoped, secretly, to be afflicted with a stomach ulcer to justify my intense anxiety and perpetual propensity to feel angry and reckless.

Quite honestly, the only thing that made my stomach feel any better that night was Ovid's work, *The Art of Love.* While I was flipping through this book I found what I needed, because the cantos that Ovid wrote in the year 23 BC were like musical keys for the piece of music I hope to play with the skill of a maestro.

Forget not the arena where mettled steeds strive for the palm of Victory. This circus, where an immense concourse of people is gathered, is very favorable to Love. There, if you would express the secret prompt-ings of your heart, there is no need for you to talk upon your fingers, or to watch for signs to tell you what is in your fair one's mind. Sit close beside her, as close as you are able; there's nothing to prevent you. The narrowness of the space compels you to press against her and, fortunately for you, compels her to acquiesce. Then, of course, you must think of some means of starting the conversation. Begin by saying the sort of thing people generally say on such occasions. Some horses are seen entering the stadium; ask her the name of their owner; and whomever she favors, you should follow suit. And when the solemn procession of the country's gods and goddesses passes along, be sure and give a rousing cheer for Venus, your protectress. If, as not infrequently befalls, a speck of dust lights on your fair one's breast, flick it off with an airy finger; and if there's nothing there, flick it off just the same; anything is good enough to serve as a pretext for paying her attention.

Be not backward in your promises; women are drawn on by promises; and swear by all the gods that you'll be as good as your word. Jove, from his high abode, looks down and laughs on lovers' perfidies.

If your mistress is ungracious and off-hand in her manner toward you, bear it with patience; she'll soon come round. If you bend a branch carefully and gently, it won't break. If you tug at it suddenly with all your might, you'll snap it off. If you let yourself go with the stream, you'll get across the river in time, but if you try to swim against the tide, you'll never do it. Patience will soften tigers and Numidian lions; and slowly and surely you may accustom the bull to the rustic plough. . . . . I do not bid thee climb, armed with thy bow, the woody heights of Maenalus, or carry heavy nets upon thy back. I do not bid thee bare thy breast to a foeman's arrows. . . . . If she's obstinate, let her have her way, and you'll get the better of her in the end. Only whatever she tells you to do, be sure you do it. Blame what she blames; like what she likes; . . . If you're playing dice, don't let her be piqued at losing, but make it look as though your luck was always out. . . . . Be sure and hold her parasol over her; and clear a way for her if she's hemmed in by the crowd; fetch a stool to help her on to the couch; and unlace or lace up the sandals on her dainty feet.

Some people would advise you to stimulate your powers with noxious herbs, such as savory, pepper mixed with thistle-seed, or yellow feverfew steeped in old wine. In my view these are nothing more nor less than poisons. The goddess, who dwells on the shady slopes of Mount Eryx, approves not such strained and violent means to the enjoyment of her pleasures. Nevertheless, you may take the white onion that comes from Megara and the stimulating plant that grows in our gardens, together with eggs, honey from Hymettus, and the apples of the lofty pine.

The curved ship is not always obedient to the same wind.

The next morning, I woke up at around eleven feeling wrecked when the phone rang. I had no desire to pick it up. I finally woke myself up and got out of bed with difficulty, my back giving me pain. Spirits from novels filled the place, sharing in sips of coffee and cigarettes. I practically had to toss Madame Bovary's ghost, who had been wallowing in my bed all night, off my pillow. Meanwhile under a warm shower, Carmen scratched my back with her wild fingers and whispered dirty words with her tongue halfway down my ear, making me lose my balance and bump my head on the side of the shower. I escaped any major casualty, cleaning the small injury on my forehead with some cologne. Before leaving the house, I made sure I had my National Library membership card with me. I had written down the names of three old manuscripts, hoping to find them there in the archives even though I was almost certain, according to my information, that two of them, "Houses of Loved Ones and Gardens of Hearts" by Ibn Fahd al-Hanbali and "The Lover's Garden and the Beloved's Promenade" by al-Kasa'i, are housed in the Ahmad III Library in Turkey, while the third manuscript, "Directing the Judicious toward the Beloved's Companionship" by Ibn Falta, is at the Egyptian National Library.

At the library catalogues, the only thing I could find regarding these manuscripts were references to them in other books from later periods. So that my trip was not a total waste of time, I borrowed two books, *The Book of the Flower* by Ibn Dawud and another one with the provocative title, *The Lovers' Quarrel*, with the hope that I would find them in complete order and not 'augmented,' like the copies I have at home.

I proceeded toward the center of the room looking for a chair. In contrast to al-Zahiriya Library, which was practically empty, this one was quite crowded. Out of the blue, I noticed a young woman whom I had run into a few times at al-Zahiriya. I headed in her direction, heeding Ovid's advice. I grabbed an empty chair and sat near her. I ventured a smile her way. I opened up *The Book of the Flower*, keeping her within sight from the corner of my eye. Then I moved my leg a few inches in her direction until I brushed her skirt, while at the very same time I turned my head toward her and said, "I've missed you so much these past few weeks that I've seen you at least twice in my dreams."

I felt strange. She got up, collecting her papers. She headed into the café adjacent to the library, so I quickly followed her there. I put down my papers, and asked her, "What are you drinking?"

"Nothing," she replied.

"I'll order two cups of coffee," I insisted.

I approached the server and told him what I wanted, then headed back to her, saying, "Coincidence is better than a thousand appointments."

"You're embarrassing me," she replied coldly.

"Why?"

"Never mind." Then she added, "Are you a graduate student?"

"No."

"Then what are you doing here?"

"I need some hard-to-find sources. And you?"

"I'm a master's student in the department of Arabic and I'm doing research on narrative methods in the Arabic literary tradition and their influence on the modern Arabic novel."

"My library is at your service," I told her. "I have tons of sources in this field. You can narrow down the issue to three or four methods."

"And what are these methods?" she asked.

I answered, "'They claimed that . . .' as in *Kalila wa Dimna* by Ibn al-Muqaffa', or 'I have heard, O king . . .' as in *A Thousand and One Nights*, 'It's said that . . .' as in maqamat, and 'The narrator said . . .' as in popular folk tales like 'The Saga of the Banu Hilal,' 'The Saga of al-Amira Dhat al-Himma,' or the 'Antara Saga.' There are many novels that imitate these styles."

Here, at this juncture, I felt lucky. She was looking at me like I was some kind of an idiot. I made the most of the situation by stretching out my hand toward the side of her mouth, as if wiping away a small speck and asked, "Are you finding any difficulty preparing your research?" She nodded her head. I tossed out another question, "Who's supervising your research?" Before she could finish his tripartite name, I uttered, "Animal," without any regret.

"You know him?" She said with surprise.

"I sometimes read his work in literary journals. He doesn't know what he's talking about. He's just a parrot in a cage of literary tradition."

She crinkled her forehead and said, "He's complicated."

"Sexually," I added.

She seemed embarrassed by this comment. "That's just my opinion. He hasn't tried to sleep with you yet, has he?"

She nodded her head in agreement. Then she looked at me assiduously. "What is it that you do, exactly?"

I replied, savoring my last sip of coffee with all the sass of a gypsy, "A novelist."

I got up and was sure that this time "the oil in the cream was not lost." I paid the bill and bid her farewell. I left proud as a peacock.

Pacing back and forth on the curb at al-Umawi Square, I waited more than seven minutes for a taxi but to no avail. Then, the 'lady of Camellia' appeared before me near the library wall. It was her. She seemed taller and more beautiful. She moved toward me, "You're still here?"

I answered immediately, "I could smell your bouquet from over two hundred meters away."

She was on the verge of laughing, "It appears you're a poet, as well."

"What do you say we walk a bit?" I asked her.

She glanced at her watch: "Okay."

We set out in the direction of al-Mahdi ibn Baraka Street. We turned down the first small street on our left. "I don't like crowded streets," I told her. Then I plucked a scent-less flower from the wall of one of the adjacent houses and put it in her hair, moving closer to her. At the end of the street I took her hand in order to cut across the road to the other direction. As soon as she set her foot on the other curb, she tried to free her hand from mine. I squeezed it strongly and then let it go. We were now next to Talitla Cafeteria. I said to her, like any seasoned Italian novelist, "What do you say we have a cappuccino?"

"Thanks, but I'm late."

"Okay. I'll take you to al-Malaki Square and we'll say our goodbyes there," I said dramatically.

Before reaching the square, I wrote down my telephone number on the newspaper that was buried in her papers, adding, "I won't sleep until I hear your voice." I hailed a taxi and opened the back door for her. Then I closed it and left after waving goodbye to her.

On my way home, I started to outline scenarios so that I could be prepared as soon as possible, especially that she would need my help on her thesis. "Leisure time," as Kundera would say, "had come to an end." We do not have any shared memories, I hardly know her. It's not that bad if she doesn't put her flour in my wicked mill: "The remnants of hard work are better than the saffron of time off." But, as a precautionary measure, as soon as I got home I dedicated myself to rereading *The Art of Hindu Love*, scrutinizing the ways in which Hindus had discovered, over three thousand years ago, the many ways to have sex. I became completely engrossed with the accompanying explanatory illustrations. While finding pleasure in the "horse method" I would then discover that the "elephant method" was both better and more intimate. In this way, I would move on to a third, fourth, and fifth method, until reaching the forty-fifth.

At the peak of my intellectual scrutiny in the anatomical sciences, the doorbell rang. I quickly shut the book and headed toward the door. Lumia was behind the peephole, though she had placed her finger over the lens before moving it. I slid open the lock (actually, there is no lock, I just like saying that, for purely literary reasons) and opened the door, half-asleep. In came Lumia, happy and carrying something wrapped in paper in her hands. She set that down on the table and hugged me, saying, "I just signed a contract for a television series. I'm playing the part of the respected sister-in-law."

"I know," I said, nodding my head.

"How?" She asked with surprise.

"The director consulted me before signing the contract with you. You know we're friends. He wanted us to reconcile after that issue we had. You, my dear miss, are now my prisoner."

She unwrapped the package, "I brought you the pizza that you love."

While I was devouring my meal, I was actually thinking about putting into practice what I had read in *The Art of Hindu Love* with Lumia. She had come of her own volition, despite our agreement a few months ago to end our relationship. She suddenly said, "If the company's headquarters weren't so close, I wouldn't have come without calling first."

"Never mind," I replied, "I've been missing you a lot."

She told me about the nature of her role in the show. It was of the weak romantic kind that TV screenwriters churn out with the greatest amount of flowery composition and hollow poetics possible. The character rarely leaves the window. And when the writer does venture to send her off to al-Sibki Park, where love affairs are often imagined, to meet her lover, she is discovered by the popcorn seller who stands behind his cart on the curb of the park and who also lives in her neighborhood. He tells her brother about the scandal and there is a heated confrontation between her and her brother and she ends up rebelling against the situation (this is how the screenwriter wrote it in the character description).

"Great," I said to her, "this role is a real model from your experience. At least you are finished with the part of the cat in the dubbed cartoon series." Then, I added, "What do you think about having a glass of wine?"

Laughing, she brought the rest of the food into the kitchen, "No, thanks. I've got my period."

This is how my relationship with Lumia flowed, with clarity and honesty. After we failed to stay together—we were just too different—an inscrutable desire erased all her faults and I became inclined to make myself available so that we could meet at any old place, or talk on the phone for almost two hours at times, as if it were a cockfight. But, in the end, we would always reconcile and make arrangements to meet the next day to take a stroll as we did in the old days.

As soon as she left, I thought about Bahija, whom I would rename 'Morning Glory.' Also, for literary reasons, I decided that this tragic fruit would need fertilizer and pruning to mature. I had not seen her with anyone or in any public place. Clearly the trench of virtuousness in which she barricades herself is merely a fragile defense mechanism, because one could not detect any trace of gunpowder nearby.

I took down three books of criticism from my library concerning the theory of the Arabic novel, narrative techniques, and the art of the maqama, as an initial surprise for her. Then I stood thoughtfully in front of a long row of novels. Love stories, in particular. I wanted to give her one as a gift, one that would leave an indelible mark on her memory.

Confronting my two choices I was stumped: *A Magian Love Story* by Abdelrahman Munif and *Samarkand* by Amin Maalouf. Both are suitable for a non-professional reader, as I gathered from her responses to my questions about novels on our first date. Then I told myself that even if the title lacks inspiration and is far less suggestive than the first, *Samarkand* is better because it is a melange of history, philosophy, and love. I rummaged around for the inspirational parts of the book and underlined those sections that had a truly positive effect on me at that time with broad strokes of my highlighter pen, especially the passage describing a passionate night the narrator spends with Shireen that is inspired by their mutual desire for a rare manuscript. It was dawn and he still had not opened its pages: "I could see it on the small night table on the other side of the bed, even though a naked Shireen was asleep with her head resting on my neck, her bare breasts alongside my ribs. Nothing in the world could make me move right now."

Around ten in the morning, I called Morning Glory, her voice mixing into the daze. She apologized for not being able to call me last night. We agreed to meet that afternoon away from the library and I promised to bring the books she needed with me. When I put down the receiver, I felt the tug of a little blue fish at the end of my line and I was sure that she would never go back to the waters she had been swimming in. Throughout the afternoon, I thought about the best ways to prepare this meal and the most inducing spices.

After inspecting Morning Glory's work on her thesis during our rendezvous at the Havana Café, the stagnant swamp she was stuck in became conspicuously clear. Especially in terms of the novels she had chosen in conjunction with her thesis advisor. But, more than that, she had not heard the names of numerous novelists from Egypt, Morocco, Libya, Saudi Arabia, and even Syria itself. It would actually be of great benefit to her if she a put into practice some of my suggestions (that is, adding some names and removing others). In order to assure the success of my imposition, I spent our entire time together discussing her research and put aside my plans for future rendezvous and intrigues. I alluded to a visit to my library so that she could peruse my treasures at her will, without forgetting Ovid's advice to touch her hand or brush her leg with my fingers while looking under the table for my lighter, which had fallen during an excitable outburst on the demise of university education.

Morning Glory shrank like a wilted rose in the face of my extensive knowledge and suggestions to develop her thesis. So, at this precise moment, I took out the novel *Samarkand* from among the books I had set on the table and said to her, "It would be best to read this novel first, as a kind of respite. It's a gift from me to you." She thanked me gratefully. I asked the waiter for the check. She attempted to open her bag to pay the bill, but I objected, taking hold of her hand to stop her from pulling out any money. I laid out the cash and we left.

She explained that her house was on the outskirts of the city and so she could not stay any later than 9:30 in the city. But she agreed to walk together for a while and mentioned how nice it would be if I accompanied her to the bus stop under al-Rayyis Bridge. We drifted in the direction of Victoria Square and then turned right. We leisurely climbed the stairs to the bridge suspended next to the bus station. Under a light drizzle of rain, I grabbed her hand, but she let it slip away. Then I hugged her, my arms wrapped around her waist with force. She tried to escape, but I grabbed her hand and held it between my fingers, saying, " Oh, that a cloud rains for you in my desert."

At the top of the stairs, she scolded me for being so reckless. I took the opportunity to ask about her romantic status. She denied having a relationship, being completely dedicated to her studies. I looked at her, certain that she was the emerald that glistened in my shiny road to heaven, even if she hid some of her secrets from me.

I stopped going to the library for the next few days, being preoccupied with rereading Calvino's advice on novel writing. At the same time, I wanted to test the strength of Morning Glory's ability to endure my absence and my ability to love again after Lumia had run off with all my emotions, turning me into a distinctly carnal being, moved only by passion and desire: a real milquetoast for Freud at those notorious philosophical conferences; sound proof of his psychoanalytical theory. It would make Marx dive under his chair, his grand stature lost forever.

Like a wild horse in a stable, I could undress women on al-Hamra Street with my mind, quickly undoing their buttons, especially those whose navels were discretely exposed. Since it made my task so easy, I never forgot to give thanks to clothing designers for creating these skintight jeans, and especially to the one whose unique vision imagined zippers in the back.

At al-Rawda Café, I would choose a strategic table, positioned to face the crystalline barrier that separates it from the very lively al-Abid Street where the young deer of my novel come together in droves. Here, I could choose from among this forest of thighs whatever I wanted, despite the café din and my engagement in heated discussions on the intifada, civil society, the Afghan war, freedom of the press, corruption, and what the next millennium might look like. All without forgetting, of course, to direct my attention to women's feet. Their toes, to be precise. For here is where a conviction I have developed over the past two years solidifies: that toes are the final measure of a woman's beauty. If a woman has ugly feet, there is no way her other attributes can compensate. Quite simply, I would write off any woman that did not conform to this theory of mine, even though I was sure that Naomi Campbell or Claudia Schiffer would never pass through al-Abid Street to go shopping at Salihiya Center. I was fascinated with international fashion magazines that devoted page after page specifically to summer shoes, and runway shows on television where silken toes slipped forward in their high heels, standing victorious, and challenging you to lift your gaze to her who possesses them. Meanwhile you are sure that she is the last princess held prisoner in the mad king's castle.

My obsession with toes reached such an unbelievable degree that I confessed the situation to a photographer I had known for a long time. I suggested that he focus his lens on toes while at hotel gala parties, but he did not quite get what I was asking of him and was even a bit disturbed by this odd tendency. And when he noticed my anger at his failure to understand the theory," he tried to make amends: "What's up with you? How am I supposed to take these pictures? Do you want me to lie under tables to get them? Should I ask people to extend one foot a bit to the right or left, like I do when I shoot faces?" Then, he added, clearly annoyed, "I would need a particular kind of lens to take these shots anyway, which I don't have." I challenged him and laid out an album filled entirely with pictures of actresses and models whose feet are clearly shown: "Get this damn lens. I will pay you double your fee for one picture." The meeting ended with my promise to set up an exhibition for him of these promised shots at the French Cultural Center.

A few days later, he set them down in front of me with pride. They were absolutely deplorable. They looked like they were taken for a medical magazine on paralysis or foot tumors. Cut off at the anklebone and not one leading up to the knee. I put the pictures back into the portfolio and threw it in his face, thanking him for his efforts with a short but lucid burst of rage, "Thank your wife for me, although she isn't up to the task. She's no Samia Gamal, or even a Fifi Abdou."

I did not have a very well laid-out plan to see Morning Glory's toes, especially since I had gotten myself in a bit of trouble by mentioning a remark that appeared just earlier: "under a light drizzle of rain." This means, quite simply, that it was winter when I became acquainted with her. Of course, she was wearing socks that covered her entire foot, assuming we ignore the presence of black socks that extend over the knees. Precision would be needed to ascertain the details. Anyhow, this is one of Italio Calvino's five recommendations. One cannot ignore it very easily, except if I had constructed another representation of our meeting, such as the heel of her boot slipping as we climbed the stairs of the bridge suspended next to the bus station, and causing her to hold on to me tightly so as not to fall. Then, she would have had to take off her boot and readjust the nails. For sure, she would not have taken off her sock, and so it follows that I would not have been able to form a true image of her toes in the semidarkness.

I was about to fall into the same absurd situation over the manuscripts housed in the Ahmad III Library in Turkey after I found an appropriate solution for getting the third manuscript at the Egyptian archives. I would commission someone traveling to Cairo to bring me back a photocopied version. A clever idea came to me to write the following sentence: "When I landed in Istanbul Airport that afternoon with the intention of getting my hands on the two lost manuscripts . . . ." But I did not finish the sentence because I was not completely sure if the Ahmad III Library was in Istanbul or Ankara. Then, what would my novelist, a pest like myself, do in Istanbul, and meanwhile I suffer a laziness that allowed me to forget my visit to Nizar Qabbani's grave that was only ten minutes from my house by taxi? So, what were you thinking, traveling to Istanbul?

The truth of the matter was that things would have kept on flowing in this direction, as if on a Persian carpet, if Lumia had not called me on her cell phone from the set. She wanted me to have her number in case I needed to call her. Before our call, which was not very clear, ended, she added, "I might stop by tonight after the shoot to talk about something important."

I hung up the phone and thought about Lumia's important matter. The phone rang again and I picked it up quickly, "Hi, Lumia." I figured her call had been cut short suddenly. The voice on the other line answered, "It's Morning Glory." I apologized for my unintentional blunder, "I'm so sorry, I was just talking with a friend in Paris and the line was suddenly cut."

"I thought I'd see you at the library today," she said.

" I was busy. How's it going?" I replied.

"I was totally engrossed with reading the novel."

"How far did you get?" I asked disinterestedly.

"I finished it yesterday. If it hadn't been so late at night, I would have called."

"You know that I stay up late. Did you like it?"

"Absolutely, it was a total pleasure. I've never read a novel like that before."

"You'll have to thank me then."

"I don't know how to thank you. I'm really glad I got to know you."

Pushing things, I said, "I want you to express your happiness in practice."

"How?"

"Something concrete."

"Concrete!" She said, a bit foolishly perhaps. "Like what?"

"Concrete like the chair that you're sitting on right now."

"But I'm in bed."

"If I were next to you right now, then I would explain it much better."

"Isn't it a bit too soon for that?"

I replied, with a dramatic tone, "I will confess to you that I've thought about you since the first time I saw you in al-Zahiriya Library. For me, that's a long time. A lifetime. When I saw you at the National Library, I said, it's Venus herself blessing this encounter."

"Venus? Who's that?"

"The goddess of love."

She laughed happily out loud. "When will I see you?"

"Right now."

"That's a bit difficult. How about tomorrow?"

"As you wish."

"Seven o'clock in front of the National Library. And don't forget to bring another novel with you."

"Kisses."

This time I could see that my boat had set sail perfectly, without any icebergs or pirate ships standing in the way, moving closer to shore and ready to drop anchor.

Once again, I found myself in a state of confusion. Confused as to what novel could carry my message perfectly into the arms of Morning Glory, without stamps complicating it or a stupid postman failing to deliver it to the right address and at the right time. I decided on Isabel Allende's novel *Aphrodite*, telling myself that it was a well-balanced meal of sexual spices. I felt sure that the dose Morning Glory had taken was working well on her. It had hit the mark exactly. After thinking a little more, though, I decided on another novel by Isabel Allende, *Paula,* because *Aphrodite* was the kind of novel one either loves from the first page or throws out the window. *Paula,* on the other hand, was a farrago of autobiography, love, and pain. It can really have an influence on a reader, especially one like Morning Glory.

I got out my highlighter pen and began searching for sections to earmark, but because I had not read this novel in a long time I could not find what I wanted easily. But I did discover what I myself would need to write my novel, particularly in the chapter where she talks about her way of writing and understanding the novel and how she wrote her first one, *The House of Spirits.* Then she talks about the circumstances surrounding writing her second one, *Of Love and Shadows.* What encouraged me most was that we (I mean Isabel and myself) resemble each other in some details. For instance, she writes in *Paula* on page 317:

> I kept writing until nighttime in the kitchen of our house in Caracas, but I wasn't getting anywhere. I had started to use an electric typewriter. . . . I try to be alone in a place that is covered in silence for long hours. I need time in order to wrestle the street noise from my head and to clean out the remembrances of life's chaos. After which I would light a candle to evoke my muses and guardian spirits and place flowers on my table to ward off boredom. I was preparing my mind and soul by way of a secret ritual to greet the first sentence while in a trance and to open a door through which I can see a glimpse of the other side and behold the cloudy frame of the story that is waiting for me.

For the first time I felt that the kitchen was an ideal place for writing. I am not the only one who writes in the kitchen. As well, for the first time I realized the beauty of the armoire where the plates are set. They resembled the shelves of a small library and the plates, the books. There is china, crystal, aluminum, clay, and plastic, even those silent spirits on the top shelf—I mean the winsome glass bottles that looked like an abstract painting, their colors mixing together both chaotically and harmoniously. Tall ones, short ones. For milk, pepper, mint, salt, sugar, tea, safflower and homemade oil. There are also coffee cups, tea cups, copper coffee makers, and a plastic container for knives and spoons that looks like a pen case, the faucet, and the garbage bin that has, in silence and with patience, borne witness to numerous drafts that I have nervously discarded into its mouth time and again.

Out of the blue, I heard the rap of Lumia's heel, with all its rage, coming down the steps. I opened the door before she rang the bell. The edge of the screenplay was sticking out of her bag. As she threw herself on the couch, she said, "I need your help."

"With what?" I asked.

She took the screenplay out of her bag, "My part in the series needs some amending. And there's no else but you to take care of this. You know what I mean?"

"Have you told the director about this?" I asked.

"He doesn't have any objection to adding some scenes. But nothing can be taken out."

"What's the nature of the scenes you want to add?"

"Haven't you read my part? There are no more than twenty scenes."

I nodded my head in agreement. She stretched out her hand and grabbed me, pulling me toward her. She wrapped her arms around me. I suddenly felt numb and let my gaze languish on her chest. My fingers danced above her open lips. She laid her head on my shoulder. I lifted mine and looked at her as if I were seeing her for the first time. I held her face in my hands and kissed her. My lips slid from her lips to her neck and then to her earlobe. "Enough," she said venomously. I opened the top button of her blouse.

"What are you doing?" She asked me in distress.

"I'm writing the requested scenes."

Now she roared, "If this is the compensation, then I don't want your help."

"Absolutely not," I said. "It's only to dive deeper into the scenes. Aren't they love scenes?"

"Yes."

"Where's the compensation, then? I'm just doing my job as best as I can."

"It's getting late. I have to go home, I have a shoot tomorrow."

"Sleep here."

"A car is coming by to pick me up in the morning. I don't want any scandals."

She got up from where she was sitting and headed toward the bathroom to fix her hair and make-up. I followed her after taking a look at her part. She was standing in front of the mirror, her clutter resting on the edge of the sink.

"Are you going to leave the screenplay with me?" I asked.

"I can do that. I have another copy of my scenes."

I was talking to her by way of the mirror while I hugged her torso. Then, I slipped my hand down to her pants button, undoing it leisurely. She was, in the meantime, busy reapplying kohl to her eyes. I had reached the bottom. She said nonchalantly, "That's enough, asshole."

I got closer, my hands firmly on her breasts. She tried, to no avail, to slip out of my arms. At last, she rested her hands on the side of the sink, dropping her head in submission. In one swift movement, executed with incredible skill, she dropped her torso back and moaned while my sightless beast thrust deeply into her dark tunnel with brute force.

After fifteen minutes of silence, Lumia ascended the steps, "When will you be done with the scenes?"

"Two days at the most," I answered.

"I'll call you in two days then," she replied, a shadow of a smile lingering on her lips.

I closed the door and headed for my bed to re-examine my 'erotic exploits' with Lumia in detail, concluding that this particular female was half holy and half whore. Of course, it was the latter half that interested me. The era of holy women concurs irrevocably with the last remnants of the nineteenth-century novel, when churches and monasteries were packed with these kinds of women begging God for mercy.

I jumped out of bed suddenly, overcome by an excitement to recover the last draft I had done of the novel. A silk thread was dangling in front of me, one that perhaps could alleviate the intense madness that had taken over me while writing. Just a second before, I had noticed a piece of wool hanging from a dust-covered tapestry on the wall opposite from where I lay. I stood directly in front of it, carefully reviewing the shapes my grandmother had woven of a gazelle's horn eighty-five years earlier. It was to be part of her wedding trousseau on condition that the weaving be accomplished by her fingers as a sign of her skill and her ability to face hardship early on in life. The woven section was the size of a saddlebag, a meter and a half long and about an arm's length wide, and was entitled, "Necklace," referring to the camel's neck. It was used as a backing for the bride's chair, after which it was filled with all of her personal belongings. My grandmother gave me this one-of-a-kind saddlebag as a gift many years ago, being that I was, at the time, one of those people who had a thing for folklore and local culture. And also, being that I was her oldest grandson whom she raised in her room for six full years, searching for lice and nits in my hair and telling me stories before bed. Overjoyed with my interest in this neglected saddlebag in the corner of her room, she led me to a trunk of her things and with shaky fingers pulled out a sack buried in the depths of the trunk. She opened it deliberately and drew out a few things: colorful pearls, seashells, shiny stones with a small hole drilled through that were used as amulets against evil spirits, a copper kohl vessel with a wooden wand, and a silver anklet. "Take what you want of your grandmother's mementos. When you marry tell your bride that these are my gift to her." She left me with the most beautiful blessing I had ever heard in my life: "Green is your path."

The saddlebag was decorated with drawings and strange shapes with clashing colors. The horse, or what appeared to be one was a scarlet red, but the palm trees, which appeared smaller than the horse, were more of a burgundy. There where geometric shapes that had never occurred to Pythagoras himself. Nevertheless, to look at the tapestry in its entirety made one feel certain that these mistakes were an essential part of the structure of the panel or scene and were envisioned before the actual weaving took place; as if everything that occurred to my grandmother while working on it (her canvas) was realizable and embodied in an imagination open to possibilities without being held accountable by any sense of reason. Milan Kundera observed in his novel *Immortality*, "It is incumbent on whomever has been granted enough madness to persevere, in this day, to write novels, to write them in a way that makes it impossible to protect their adaptability. In other words, making them insusceptible to being narrated." He adds, mocking the interchangeable structure of traditional novels, "Unfortunately, most novels written these days, are bound, more than they need to be, to a singular fundament of action. What I mean is that all of them are based on one causative chain of acts and events. These novels resemble a narrow street that the characters pass straight through while being lashed along the way. Dramatic tension is the actual curse of the novel, because it turns everything, every page, scene, and most shocking observation into a mere stage leading to the final denouement where the meaning of all that came before it is concentrated. If a novel is inspired by a spark of tension, then it will perish like a straw belt."

I wrote in my notebook (which had become like a war map), "My grandmother is the greatest novelist in the world, weaving all of her dreams and cryptic codes into a gazelle's horn and then taking an everlasting break."

It was now well past midnight and I had lost all contact with my inspirational demons. I got dressed quickly and went out to roam the streets. I stopped in a crappy bar called Faridy that resembled an auto repair shop. As soon as I opened the door, I noticed an old alcoholic friend of mine, his elbow propped on the table, perhaps in case its corroded sides crumbled beneath him. I entered and pulled up a chair across from him. He was happy to see me and poured me a glass of Syrian wine, then took out a handful of white pumpkin seeds from his bag and set them on an empty plate. "You finished work early," I said to him.

"I never went in the first place," he replied.

This friend of mine had the oddest job in the world and it remained a source of mockery among his friends. Every night, he was required to make a tour of the airport road to take account of the number of broken streetlights, for the protection of travelers and in particular official entourages, and to record the location of the damaged ones. What caused the most mockery is that he was drunk all day and night, and his lights were out all the time.

Abruptly, he raised his glass and said, "How far have you gotten with your toe theory? Honestly, it's a profound one." Then, he added, "I'm quite sure that we will soon evolve into a party for the masses."

"How?" I asked.

"Because of the slogan that we're choosing for our party. What do you think? 'To be a leg for a barefoot woman.' Do you know that the masses, from the Atlantic to the Gulf, thirst for such a glittery and sexy slogan?"

I said to him amusingly, "From this moment on, I consider you the secretary general of this party."

He raised his glass and said, "To the health of the party's theorizer."

His left eye was partly closed all the while we talked. Pointing out the dark circle underneath it, I asked, "What's with your eye?"

Laughing, he replied, "It's a party secret that I don't like to divulge to anyone in times like these."

"But I'm not just anyone."

After pouring what was left in his glass down his throat, he said, "You know the magnitude of my excitement for the party's theory ever since you explained it to me a few months ago. And since last summer, I have been the reigning king on al-Hamra Street and at Salihiya

Shopping Center. I even expanded to Bab Tuma Street and the area of al-Qassa', contemplating the princesses' toes with indescribable obsession. But my ardor has diminished these days because of our cursed winter that forbade me to enjoy the view, for objective reasons, until it led me to a devilish idea: to stand in front the windows of women's shoe stores. This has become a second job for me. For an hour or two every day, I wallow in the most beautiful feet of the season and record my observations on the importance of the middle toe and the little one; the beauty of the foot; and the influence of the second toe on the splendor of the foot as a whole, to the point where I began harassing a woman by praising her toes. She lured me into a neighboring street. Meanwhile I thought that this matter of mine had finally led to its climax. But as she got into her car she introduced me to her personal driver who was standing on the corner waiting for her. What happened, happened." Then, he added, "In any event, I don't regret a thing," and pouring another glass, he said, "You can consider me the party's first living martyr."

I went home alone, leaving the secretary general of the party asleep on the table, and thought first about Morning Glory, and then about Lumia and the screenplay laying on the couch. I leafed through Lumia's part quickly and wrote down in pencil some ideas for scenes that ought to be added between the ones already there. I would flesh them out in the morning. I felt like De

Bruyn's donkey, who remained confused between two women until he lost both of them. I pleaded out loud, "If God wanted to destroy the ant, he would have given her wings." Then I went over my plan to end my relationship with Lumia. A bird in the hand is better than a crane in flight. Perhaps some of you will notice that I am using proverbs a lot at this time. The reason is not so much related to early morning wisdom as it is simply to my sudden awareness of what is written on the almanac hanging behind me on the kitchen wall and the fact that I have started to jot down proverbs that appeal to me as I sit by them at the table on which I write this novel. In order to ease some of the disarray since my inspirational demons deserted me, I have come to a sensible determination regarding both Lumia and Morning Glory. While Morning Glory may merely be a very short story, Lumia, on the other hand, is a long novel. I do not think that a sensible person would put all of his eggs in a basket of the (very short story) kind and let dust cover the pages of a wanton novel like Lumia. On this basis, I crossed out a proverb I had been intending to capitalize on during this sticky situation: Whoever eats from two tables, chokes. Using all the power vested in me for rational thought, I decided to open my appetite to what is delicious and tasty from both tables, with all the vigor of a captain facing a fierce storm without doubting for a moment that his ship will be saved in the end, even if its sails fall. There wasn't one I wouldn't write about.

With this ruthless spirit, I left for my rendezvous with Morning Glory, making a minor adjustment to my previous plan. I swapped *Paula* for a novel that I felt would expedite the process of closing the gap between us. *In Praise of the Stepmother* is by the greatest erotic writer, whom, sadly, we almost lost when he declared his candidacy for president in Peru a few years back. Luckily, Mario Vargas Llosa lost the election. I never tire of finding relevant parts or using my highlighter pen. And so I did not need to venture too far into the novel. When I aim my rifle, I always find a rabbit or gazelle through the scope. Early in the book I landed on these scattered pearls:

> She left her left hand on Don Rigoberto's stomach, although what it actually touched was a human mast, erect and throbbing. . . . At the depth of this sweet storm she had become, she had found life, as if she were appearing and disappearing in a mirror that is losing its glow, at times outlining a face, that of a cherub . . . . She moaned in pain and pleasure, and in a warbled whirlwind she saw an image of Saint Sebastian pierced by arrows, crucified and soaked. She felt as if she were being stabbed right in the middle of her heart.

Looking over the cover of *In Praise of the Stepmother,* Morning Glory said, "It looks like a romantic novel." It depicts Venus, naked from the waist up, in an embrace with Cupid. A detail from a painting of the Mannerist period.

I said, "It has nothing to do with romanticism."

"Anyway, do you like Gibran Khalil Gibran?" she asked.

"I think there are some things that a person does once in his life, like getting vaccinated for polio or tuberculosis. I read *Broken Wings* in junior high school. I remember it leaving a good impression on me that I don't imagine would be the same today," I said with disappointment.

I found this to be an opportunity to cleanse her mind of whatever was left over from novels whose only outstanding features are the glossy paper they are printed on and the massive output of their authors, who appear, time and again, in newspapers and on television, and in this way reaffirm the importance of enjoyment and congeniality in any literary work. In an attempt to close in on my endgame, I said, "Take the novel *Samarkand*, for example. Didn't you read it with pleasure and fascination?"

"Of course," she said. "But it's a bit pornographic."

Digging a hole with my toe in the ground where she stood, I responded, "Like the character Shireen. Isn't she wonderful?"

She replied, a bit confused, "Sure."

"The novelist should not be a preacher," I said.

Sweet flakes of wisdom mixed with virtuous honey fill shops, prayer rooms, and monasteries. But life, well, it's somewhere else, and I knew that she was now like a wet duck who had just left an ice-covered lake.

"What do you say we walk for a bit?" I asked.

She got up immediately, still contemplating the charm of the al-Shaykh Muhyi al-Din suq where we had a tasty meal of fuul. I pointed out an old mosque across the way from us. I said, "Here is where al-Shaykh Muhyi al-Din ibn Arabi lies. The greatest Sufi philosopher." Then we headed toward downtown. When we hit al-Abyad Bridge Square, we turned into a narrow alleyway. She was taken by surprise when I squeezed her fingers, tucked securely in the pocket of her long coat. And just as I had calculated in my mind, we suddenly found ourselves right in front of my house. "This is where I live," I said. "How about a cup of hot tea?" She turned it down, saying she would be late getting home to the suburbs. Pulling her by hand to the stairs, I reassured her, "You won't be late. It's an opportunity for you to look over my library." I had opened the door and put my hand in hers nudging her gently inside. I closed the door and turned on the light.

Studying the posters and pictures on the walls, she said, " Your house is homey."

"That's because a dove like yourself fluttered its wings among its walls," I replied.

My library was spread out between the living room, bedroom, and kitchen, in between seat cushions and on top of the refrigerator. It was a kind of labyrinth of books. I hit a button on the tape recorder and the rhythmic sounds of Rabi' Abu Khalil's songs filled the room. Morning Glory was still standing in the middle of the living room, a bit perplexed, despite her unseen delight. I instructed her, "Sit, while I make some tea."

"You don't have to," she said.

"A glass of juice, then?" She nodded her head, flipping the pages of the novel *Honor* by Sonallah Ibrahim.

I busied myself with making the juice quickly: two oranges, a lemon, and a pomegranate. Then I added a dash of gin and mixed it all together. Meanwhile a little fly of passion buzzed potently in my head.

Taking the glass, she said, "I haven't read anything by this author before."

"But he's well known. He's achieved a widespread fame since his first novel *The Smell of It*, and then with *The Committee*."

I sat across from her, "How far have you gotten with your master's thesis?"

"After listening to what you had to say, I feel that it needs more focus. But the problem is that my thesis supervisor has stipulated that I write only on certain novels."

"The most important thing is that you graduate. After that, you can throw half of these novels into the garbage."

"That's what I'll do. But, now, I've got to go."

When she made her move to get up, I grabbed her arm and wrapped myself around her, pulling her forcefully to my chest.

"What are you doing?" she said. "I don't believe this. I didn't expect this kind of behavior from you."

Searching for her lips, I replied, "I can't fight your charm any more."

I put my mouth on her lips and threw her down on the couch revitalized. Her defensive armies were in retreat, she had started to surrender. I touched her cheek with my fingers. Her neck. She closed her eyes. I slid down to her chest. Her thighs. Her garden. She grabbed my hand forcefully and moved it away. Not by choice, I returned to her high hills and discovered hidden treasures in areas that I had passed by too quickly before. I whispered in her ear, "Are you Shireen or Morning Glory?" Meanwhile, my other hand was removing her shoe, caressing, with the expertise of a jeweler, her toes through her translucent black silk stockings.

When I opened my eyes in the dark, I had no idea what time it was. But I knew it was night. I turned on the light and looked at my watch. It was 10:20. My head was spinning. Had I actually met Morning Glory or did I miss our rendezvous?

I made a cup of coffee and smoked three cigarettes.

I tried to remember what I had seen in my dream. But I could not recall anything except one detail: that the ink in the pen that I use to write my novel had dried up. I looked for the pen. I tried it. It was fine. The only way I could explain this dream was that my imagination would dry up soon, even though the characters and events were following me everywhere. I almost believed I was truly a novelist. More than that, I had a feeling that I would surprise the literary milieu with a work "unparalleled for its time," without a tinge of regret. No, instead, my delusions led me to even more precarious mountains, putting me face to face with "my dear reader" in my role as that charming creator of the text that enjoys an inscrutable respect from new readers who have a burning desire to meet personally, if only once, with this craftsman. What they expect is him in the flesh who combines the brains that created Doctor Faustus, Tom Jones, and Candide (I almost added my novel to the end of this line even though I have yet to lay down an appropriate title for my daily delirium). What dissuaded my resolve to end these nightly ruminations was Alberto Manguel's explication which I read in his enjoyable book on the history of reading in the chapter, "The Writer as Reader." He writes, "Seven copies were sold." So thought the hero of the novel *Nightmare Abbey*, by Thomas Love Peacock, published in 1818. "Seven is a mystical number, it is a good omen. I need to follow up on the effect of these seven copies on the buyers who will become the seven golden torches that light up the world in front of me."

I thought about the miserable fate that awaited my novel. But, in that moment of dark confusion, there is a light, based on real life, before me. An old friend works as an accountant in one of the agricultural banks.

He has rather good expertise in distributing books of all types: literary, medical, technical, or scientific, by making them one of the required papers to a long line of farmers, who arrive in the morning and leave in the afternoon, that must be submitted before a loan is distributed. Under the arm of each applicant is a copy of at least one of these wondrous books. Meanwhile they have no idea why they are required to accept this commodity. They cannot read, so they suffice with glancing at the pictures of the authors, each of whom rests his right cheek on a fist on the back cover of a book, without, unfortunately, having found anyone to slap him on the left cheek before he destroys other helpless new readers.

I was even surer of this because one of the authors, of them who write superfluous prose, actually achieved massive success. A gaseous odor emanated from him, the result of a rhetoric cooked in ghee. His last novel sold thanks only to a stern memo from public agencies to acquire this dead weight. Thousands of copies in three successive printings found their way quite easily to the warehouses of associations for cement and iron cable, fodder, poultry, grain, mills, a tire company, and other obscure places. I heard that he signed a contract to turn the novel into a television series (thirty episodes). These days he drinks yerba mate on the balcony of his new house, his stomach bubbling with new destructive gases that he has considered releasing as soon as the

Afghan war ends, when he is sure of Bin Laden's fate, something that worries him a bit.

I was on the verge of sending the first freight load of my novel by way of Qadmous Tours offices. If it had not been for the incessant ringing of my phone (which made me curse modern inventions as I picked up the receiver), then a thousand copies by express mail would have been enough for readers out in the districts.

It was Lumia on the line, setting her mind at ease as to the fate of the scenes that should have been completed by now. I told her, "They're ready. You can pass by any time." Then, I added slyly, "Even if it's after midnight."

Laughing, she replied, "You're dreaming."

"You're joking," I said.

"Listen," she went on. "I have a shoot tomorrow in an old traditional house in Bab Tuma. What do you think about meeting there?"

"Sure. I'll wait for your call tomorrow."

I hung up the phone and picked up the screenplay, heading into the kitchen. In half an hour I banged out six average-length scenes. Three of them take place in the garden and two in a microbus taxi. The last scene is a monologue in the room, one that Lady Macbeth would not dare to utter. It revolves around betrayal and deception. Then I numbered the scenes and slipped them into the screenplay, determined that she would be pleased with what I had written compared to the chatter that already choked the text. It was as if I were saying, "There is no reward for him who grinds flour well."

On my way to Bab Tuma, I dropped off a draft of my novel at a typesetter, with the idea of reviewing it afterward on a computer and pruning the noxious weeds that had crept into it. And to add any sentences, commas, and enumeration deemed necessary. But as soon as I left it at the office, I was a mess because I felt that some of the lecherous sections scattered throughout the work could offend the young woman who had taken on the project of copying the draft. To make matters worse, she wore a headscarf. I got a hold of myself, saying, "No doubt, she's used to the novelist's mind. And who's to say that she's not in charge of typing and printing out readers' books for elementary classes. You need to forget the whole thing. It's her problem anyway. She's not working for free." As I walked into the alley where the shoot was taking place, I told myself, "Perhaps I've even freed her from a grievous discontent after having typed a book on globalization or combating desertification."

I waited for about half an hour for Lumia to finish shooting silent extra scenes for the character that she plays in the series. I was watching her on the monitor. My eyes focused on the movement of her firm lips during these repetitive and numerous takes, taken because of the director's orders or technical mistakes. Lips with the taste of honey-dipped milk, exactly as I had whispered into her ear long ago at the moment of revelation that swept away her might and the obstinacy that she clung to and which was transformed, after a few months, into a jealousy that shackled the two of us irrevocably. It took the form of revenge and hatred at times, and the madness of passionate love at others, until I was completely cured of her love. I knew that there was no hope for a love like this to continue. But the scent of mutual desire remained a secret between us.

We left the shoot and went to a nearby bar. Out of the blue she said, "The most beautiful thing about you is your barbarity."

"That's because you are, quite simply, a masochist of the most refined type." I replied. Then, I added, "Anyway I'm at your service for only twenty-four hours a day."

"Braggart," she said while pouring another glass of beer.

"In any event, this proposition is for a limited time only because these days I'm living a different love story."

"You!" she said sarcastically.

"What about it?" Then I added, blowing my cigarette smoke toward her, "We novelists, my young lady, are not able to live without love stories because they are the fuel that lights the imagination and determines the fates of the characters."

"So simple," she said disapprovingly, "we novelists! And since when have you been so audacious? You said you were going to write a television series. What's going on with that?"

"Television series are written for the entertainment of housewives, and this isn't what I'm into."

"How are you going to take care of your ever-growing debts?"

"From the sales of my novel. And in the worst-case scenario the Su'ad al-Sabah Prize will take care of things."

This time, she was serious, "But really, the series idea that you told me about a while back was a really good one. And if you do write it, production companies will snatch it up."

"Forget about it."

"Really, you're making me sad."

I digressed (I had just finished reading Herman Hesse's memoir), "Every artist must start his journey across the hell of his own consciousness in order to quell the anarchy of his soul in the kingdom of the eternal spirit."

"Spare me your spirituality, right now."

"When you read *Siddhartha* you will change your mind."

"You are like a Steppenwolf. Aren't you happy with this novel."

"Of course, but, 'every situation has a saying.'"

"You're talking to me as if I don't know you."

I took a piece of paper out of my pocket on which I had written a story that I liked. I said, "Listen to this story: It happened in Baghdad that an elderly man married his daughter to a cobbler. On their wedding night, the cobbler, drunk, bit the young girl's lips until they bled. The following morning the father saw the wound and said, 'Was it necessary to dig your teeth into my daughter as you do into shoe leather? Don't do more than this. I'm not joking. When there's a struggle during sex, only death can eradicate its scars.'"

With victory in her eye, she retorted, "What's important is that you used the word sex. Isn't that so? Just be yourself and forget the kingdom of the eternal spirit."

"I know I have been like the cobbler with you."

"The time for this kind of talk has passed."

"Try me."

"I'll pay the bill," she said as she got up.

I spent a long respite in the bed of spiritual love, moving between a number of gardens: Jalal al-Din al-Rumi, Sa'adi al-Shirazi, Farid al-Din al-Attar, Ibn al-Farid, and al-Hallaj. I would sip the Orphic wine and dive into the meaning of the soul without arriving at any certitude resounding with a mystical voice. Here are some passages from Jalal al-Din al-Rumi's al-Nay qasida:

> The artist rips a reed out from a thicket of canes.
> He drills a few holes and then gives it a name.
> Ever since, it wails from a pain aching of separation,
> Forgetting the practiced act that gave it the life of
> a nay.

In my mind, I hobbled over to Farid al-Din al-Attar's shop proposing to help him copy his one hundred and fourteen manuscripts. I started earnestly on a copy of *Conference of the Birds* and *The Secrets of a Sleeping Woman*. Meanwhile my master was preoccupied with treating his illness with rose essence. I continued doing this until I witnessed his death in Nishapour at the hands of the Mongols in 1220. Quite miraculously, I was able to save thirty of his manuscripts from the ravages of fire. In Shiraz, I accompanied Hafiz al-Shirazi to meet Tamerlane after his attack on the city that killed seven thousand inhabitants. Hafiz greeted him with lines from one of his qasidas: "If al-Hasna' had received me, then I would remit her, instead of her spinster sisters Samarkand and Bukhara." This made Tamerlane rage, "With my burnished sword I have subjugated most of the world. You are an unlucky and miserable poet who's selling my city and the base of my kingdom for the empty space on a young girl's cheek!"

Hafiz responded, bowing his head respectfully, "You're right. It's because of these frivolous expenditures that I have fallen to the miserable condition that you find me in now." He asked for forgiveness and offered him a present. When the time of his death arrived, I was appointed guardian of his tomb. It had gotten to be that whenever I found the ground of the tomb destroyed, I would rebuild it. I would explain to the public that my master Shams al-Din Hafiz al-Shirazi was not a perverse poet like they thought. Rather he understood the power of the senses to kindle the fire of love in dead hearts. Once he entered the labyrinth of existence, he would extricate the truth of the body. You cannot see the hidden pearls in his poetry, because you are content to gaze upon the shell only. And so it became customary for some people to go to his tomb with great veneration, opening his diwan of poetry howsoever it was agreed upon to find an answer to his obscure musings. I was there one night with a candle copying amulets for a disciple of my master, like this one:

> Are desire and longing all what one finds in love?
> Your dagger is better than the one I have.
> I have made my head a shield
> From the ointment of others.
> Don't pull on the knight's reins,
> And don't hand him his reins.
> Fasten me with precision to the saddle's thong
> That you use for pure pleasure.
> When dust from your doorstep falls
> On my head, they will say: Hafiz was crowned king.

In a corner of the great Sheikh Muhyi al-Din ibn Arabi's tomb, I chose a place to watch visitors. At times I would dive into the pages of *The Mecca Victories*, at others, I would augment my conviction with "All that does not become feminine, may not be relied upon."

And when I finished the treatises, I read *The Interpreter of Desire* and knelt in front of his tomb, repeating:

> My heart started to welcome every image
> Such that, a pasture is for gazelle and a monastery
>   for monks,
> A house is for idols, and the Ka'ba of Ta'if,
> The tablets of the Torah, and the pages of the Quran . . .

until I slept for one year. When I woke up, I found myself in the presence of al-Nirfari, who was saying to me, "Oh, servant [of God], the letter [of the alphabet] is my fire. The letter is the storehouse of my secret."

Then he said to me, "I was learned, there is no contradicting it. I was ignorant, there is no contradicting this. I am not of the earth or of the sky."

"If you see fire, stand in it. You will not burn. For if you stand in it, it will go out. But if you run from it it will follow you and burn you."

"The value of each person is the speech of his heart."

"The act of the heart originates as an act of the body."

"Every loved one yearns, even if he is united."

In front of the barber's mirror, I contemplated my beard (that had grown long), my hollow, sunken eyes, and my overall shabby condition. I knew that I had failed to traverse the wilderness of the spirit and that my solitude had taught me speech more than it did silence or introspection. I also realized that my fate lies in knowledge of the body first and foremost and that spirituality emanates from the dust of the body, not from the clouds high above. Suddenly, I had an increased desire to see Morning Glory. Quickly I fixed the nick that the blade left on the bottom of my chin and put my clothes on like a fox leaving a cemetery that has picked up a scent. I waited in the rain for my beloved. She never arrived. Without losing hope, I headed for a telephone booth on the corner of the street to call my ladylove. I sensed a silvery ring emanating from the 'hello' she so calmly uttered. I replied, "The rain reminded me of you."

"You!"

"I want to see you now, " I said.

"I can't go out in this kind of weather. Anyway, I don't want to see you."

I sensed a tremor in her voice, ìIt's your fate that we meet.î

ìIt's your fate to wait until tomorrow.î

"But I miss you more than you can imagine."

"I'm afraid of you."

I read a slogan posted on the glass of the booth, "Soar with al-Buraq." I said to her, "If I had wings, then I would tap on your bedroom window with them . . ." And at this clumsy revelation, the line was cut. I searched my pockets for a coin with which to complete the call, but didn't find one. I promised myself I would finish what I had to say when I got home.

As I walked in the rain, empty taxis passed, heading toward Jawaharlal Nehru Street, accompanied by specters of the characters in my novel, their features unfinished. It was mostly Morning Glory who perplexed me after I had singled her out so decisively in the novel. I had gone quite far without finding any convincing angle for her wielding so much power. I realized that I was essentially comparing her with Lumia. If I suppose (from what is left of my spiritual inheritance) that she is the spirit, and Lumia the body, then the reader will spit in my face when he discovers, suddenly, that I am one of the descendants of al-Shahrurdi after all this brazenness with Lumia.

I was now sure about the integrity regarding the issue of Lumia, because as I returned to write, I immediately rendered seven pages without finding one appropriate expression to complement what I had written a few days earlier about the smell of wild mint emanating from Morning Glory's underarms, because the truth of the matter is that I had never actually accessed this precarious region. I was almost able to caress her breasts from the outside of her wool sweater. Worse than all this, the pen that I wrote with had completely dried out and I could not write with any of the other pens that I tried one after another in vain.

Exasperated, I left my papers. I was overcome with a strong feeling that fate was holding out. I lit a cigarette, setting it in the corner of my mouth like Hanna Mina. I started pacing in front of the kitchen window to get hold of some new ideas, but an intense smell of frying eggplant emanated from a neighbor's kitchen, compelling me to leave my office immediately. I headed into the living room. My zeal to call Morning Glory abated as I became preoccupied with watching a report being aired on Al Jazeera on the situation of Afghans after the end of Taliban rule, in which television cameras focused on the barbers of Kabul at the moments following the Taliban's fall from power and on its oppression. How often the body becomes a site of tyranny, as they strengthen their grip on spirits and minds. Shaving one's beard became suspicious to the point of approaching an act of disobedience and puts whomever reaches his hand to his chin in a position of political opposition. And Afghan women. Saved from the strangest piece of clothing that the human mind could ever have imagined, tantamount to a tent that completely covered a woman's body save some holes on the face, for some kind of ventilation, as if she had just left an apiary.

When the report ended, I turned off the television. I was overwhelmed with the feeling that the world was on its way to its inevitable death; that the entirety of human culture and civilization was living in the barbaric splendor of the Middle Ages, except armed with the most modern tools of killing and destruction in order to eradicate all the mystified souls, wherever they may be, merely because of a difference of opinion or belief. I, personally, do not differ much from the infernal

American machinery in my reckless attempts to force Morning Glory out of the secret cave she's hiding in. She had raised a white flag, surrendering with complete abandon in the face of my maniacal desire.

To stop dragging out these delusions any further, I picked up a book on chaste love that was perched above the desk. It had become like a reference book for my novel. I leafed through it, bored. Then I looked in the index for something to pique my interest. I looked up a short chapter on the poet Majnun Layla, but as soon as I read the first line, I felt bored once again. With hollow rhetoric, the author attempted to praise the poets of chaste love and dislodge any suspicion of latent desire in their lives. He would ignore qasidas whose inglorious meanings lay hidden in their texts in order to structure a conclusion based on his introduction, which was stuffed with drippy, syrupy sweets. Especially since other reasonable academic studies have claimed that the chastity of these poets was much more a coercive than a spiritual or philosophical choice. Indeed, it was not enough for Majnun Layla to just hang around the school wall where Layla studied syntax and rhetoric. Not in the least. Actually, he was quite vulgar around his peers, such as Umar ibn Abi Rabi'a, Urwa ibn Hizam, and Jamil Buthayna. Moreover, he would slip into her 'territory' every time the opportunity arose. Especially on Thursdays when her parents went to the movies to watch their favorite film. I think it was *Gone with the*

Wind. Layla had to hide him more than once in the maid's bed when she was surprised by her father's early return from the café, sparks shooting from his eyes. Immediately after a young colleague from the Amiri tribe or the Bani Uthra objected to her being at a backgammon match, Layla was placed in an unenviable and difficult position.

An intriguing story told by the poet Sa'adi al-Shirazi on the life of al-Majnun helped to abate my ire: The king of the Arabs heard the story of Majnun and his love for Layla, so he invited him to his court and asked him, "What did you see in her that you started to forget yourself, injuring your hand when peeling an orange?" Majnun answered, "How nice it would be that I could see her."

The king searched and brought forth Layla. She was slim, brown-skinned, and less attractive than his eastern neighbors. Majnun said, "Oh, one should see her from my eye's window. There is a big difference between taking a pinch of salt by hand and pouring it on the wound."

I do not think that Majnun's response meant that he merely intended to gaze upon her from afar while she was busy rekindling the fire to boil the camel's milk.

The first thing I did after reading this story was to look for my notebook and jot it down with a pencil I had found on the nightstand. It occurred to me to tell Morning Glory this story in an appropriate context so that she could come to understand that I am Majnun and she, Layla, of course. Then I dropped the idea completely, afraid of any confusion on her part that would lead us to talk about Uthri poetry and its aesthetics. This would not help steer my ship, with all its power, to another shore, especially since Morning Glory, as I suspected, would have finished reading *In Praise of the Stepmother*. I decided to steer the ship's rudder in light of her personal discoveries.

About an hour and an half before my rendezvous with her, I made a tour of the stationery stores to buy a black pen exactly like the one I was using before. I bought three, trying them out first in the store, afraid they might not work. I also bought a ream of paper, a new highlighter, and some red pens. I chose a pen in the shape of a laughing duck as a symbolic gift for my beloved. The magical imagination of those Japanese who invent all these different kinds of pens and stationery tools never ceased to amaze me. It made me think seriously.

I wonder what kind of pen Yasunari Kawabata used when he wrote his famous novel, *The House of the Sleeping Beauties*. By the way, this is the one novel that Marquez wishes he could have written. Then I imagined that I was a writer during the Abbasid period. How I would have endured writing on coarse paper made from tree bark or on a piece of camel or gazelle hide, clasping my cane quill from its jar and dipping it into the inkwell that receives the tip, fabricated from anemones, violets, birds of paradise, and other wild unnamed flowers that have been crushed and boiled in large pots before taking on their final form, placed in small vessels in the shops of scribes, the caliph's salon, and the locales of engravers (those who would fabricate their own secret colors that only they knew, leaving behind a mark or trace that would point to this or that engraver). It could be an insignificant flower, the fold of a woman's scarf, an undetectable movement in a horse's feet, the elongation of the letter *mim* in a Quranic verse, or an intriguing epigram that confirms the truth in "Calligraphy is the language of the hand."

On this trajectory, I stumbled upon Ibn al-Bawwab and his school of calligraphy where the craft is taught by the sheikh of all calligraphers, Abu Ali ibn Muqlah. He was absorbed in copying the holy Quran for the sixty-fourth time in the Rihani script. The copies were gifted to Sultan Selim I, who them handed over to the Laleli Mosque in Constantinople. A copy of the Rihani script with his signature can be found today in the Chester Beatty Library in Dublin.

As for his method of working, he describes it by saying, "It should be that the letters appear connected, disconnected, abstruse, and open in their best form and their most splendid nature containing the parts in their proximity and their collectivity." He also tells of something that happened to him when he had recourse to the storehouse of books commissioned by Baha al-Dawla ibn Adud al-Dawla in Shiraz:

One day I saw an edition of a collection covered in black in a completely neglected book storehouse in Shiraz. I opened it. It was one part of [the] thirty [parts] of the Quran recorded by the calligrapher Abu Ali ibn Muqlah. I liked it and set it aside. I did not stop searching high and low for every part mixed in all the books until I collected twenty-nine parts, leaving only one. I searched the storehouse endlessly, but could not find it. I learned that the volume was missing, so I singled it out and went to Baha al-Dawla to tell him the story. He said, "Complete it for me." I said, "I am at your disposal, on the condition that if you pass over the missing part and you do not recognize it, then you are to give me a robe of honor and a hundred dinars." He said, "I agree." I took the volume from his hands and left for my house. I entered the storehouse and flipped through old manuscripts and what looked like another manuscript of the volume. There were all kinds of paper, Samarkandi and ancient Chinese, all wonderfully elegant. I took the papers that corresponded to what I was looking for and wrote down the part. I gilded it, rendering the gold to look old. I extracted some leather and bound it. Then I handed the complete volume to Baha al-Dawla who flipped through it section by section, not stopping at that which was done by my own hand. Then he said to me, "Which is the part done by your hand?" I replied, "You will not know which it is, so that its value will not diminish in your eyes. This is a complete volume by the hand of Abu Ali ibn Muqlah. Let's keep it our secret." He said, "Done."

Ah, indeed the secret, I said to myself after taking a spot alongside the door at the café waiting for Morning Glory. I wondered: What secret will I hide in the web of my novel? With what loom will I spin something so enticing that the reader will jump from his place and scream, "This is it, man!" Shahrazad was hiding an extremely lucrative talent, the art of storytelling. Look, Ibn al-Bawwab asked his benefactor Baha al-Dawla to hide the secret of the greatest act of textual transgression that ever took place in the fifth century Hijri.

Even Abu Subhi al-Tinawi, the Damascene painter famous for his primitive canvases inspired by popular folk heroes like Antara and Abla and al-Zahir Baybars, had a special secret drawn into Anatara's mustache, Abla's eyebrows, or the sword of al-Zayr Salim Abu Layla al-Muhalhal that no one could detect. When there was not enough room on the glass panel to accommodate the tail of Antara's horse, he, quite simply and without any thought to the rules of perspective, would draw it in any empty spot that he could find on the panel. It was his private kingdom. And perhaps due to a previous experience when drawing Noah's Ark, on the stern of this wondrous ship he learned how it was possible for one to place different kinds of creatures in a limited space such that there was absolutely no problem of where to set the crow or the snake or the olive branch.

But, in terms of the trade secret that Abu Subhi al-Tinawi had hidden for seventy-seven years, he never revealed it to anyone until a few months before his death. One early July morning in the year 1973, he sensed the end was near. So he called his children to his small shop in a narrow alley in the Bab al-Jabiya neighborhood. There, in the midst of the smell of paints, inscrutable scents, and the humidity of the walls, he bid farewell, with reverence and for the last time, to his characters. Without uttering a word, he took up his brush and started to copy the panel "Antara and Abla," reflecting on the precise slope of the lines of Antara's horse and the eyes of Abla's horse in the first panel he drew, so that he could reproduce what he had done before. This is the first secret he revealed. Whoever reflects on his work would think that al-Tinawi was drawing from memory and imagination each time in a different way than what he had done previously. When he finished his preliminary sketches of the heroes' features he would start to mix the colors and fill in the empty forms with them. While decorating Abla's saddle and the taut brow-band above the horse's blaze, he created a small flower with a red heart just a few centimeters from Abla's head. From under the gold-embroidered cloak that Antara's beloved was wearing, the fingers of her left hand jumped out to grab the horse's halter, painted red. And with impetuous fingers, the line of Antara's mustache was bent upward with an ashen black.

When he felt completely confident with what he had crafted with his own two hands, he wiped down his brushes and cleaned them of any color. Then he would dip one anew in a dark brown and write on the lower half of the panel in the space between two feet of Abla's horse: "Syria - Damascus - Abu Subhi al-Tinawi - Bab al-Jadiya - the Hindu korner (corner)."

Before the wonder of his children and their dismay at the difficulty of this profession, he had pulled out his trade secret, or more precisely, the secret of his special signature that no one else has discovered, save his children, to this day. As he was leaving, he stood at the threshold of his little shop and turned back to say one thing, "I recommend that you never forget the wisdom and gallantry of these heroic characters. If one of you senses a broken spirit in the eyes of Antara or even his horse's, then you must rip up the canvas and start drawing it afresh."

Just as I was leaving that narrow alley in Bab al-Jadiya, wide enough for al-Zahir Baybars' entourage to pass through, Morning Glory walked in, heading for my table and wearing a smile that betrayed a secret understanding she had made with the fox (of my plan) who had been caught in the chicken coop. She said to me immediately, "Were you expecting me to come after being a half hour late?" I replied with all the serenity of haiku poets, "I would wait a lifetime for you, dear glory of my life."

Tossing the novel *In Praise of the Stepmother* onto my lap like a poisonous spider, she said, "This time I think you made a mistake."

I replied, decisively, "On the contrary, it's a philosophical novel. It's been translated into nineteen languages worldwide. This is a conclusive sign that what you consider depraved, as what I gathered from your childish behavior, is only a bridge to the discovery of the ruins of the human soul and the crushing of spiritual revolts in the face of the brutal conditions that mark twentieth-century civilization." Then I added, "It's unfortunate that someone like you, working on a master's, understands things on such a superficial level." And, while stirring the sugar in my tea, "For your information, young lady, the author of this novel was a candidate for president in his country, not for a pimp in a brothel."

At this point, I stopped my attack, lit a cigarette, and turned my face with indignation toward the window, viewing the motion of the street.

After being soaked to the bone by my downpour, she said with a sense of urgency, "I'm sorry. I didn't mean to insult you. But I'm not used to novels like this."

"It would have been better if I had given you 'perfume novels' rather than worldly ones like this."

Laughing, she said, "It's not as bad as that. Anyway, have you brought me a new one?"

"No."

"Why not?"

"I decided to leave things in your hands."

"What do you mean?"

"I don't know what you like to read."

"If you're mad at me, then I'll leave right now."

"Whatever you want."

"Then I'd like you to take me to the bus station. Would you refuse me?"

Clasping her hand, I said, "Drink your coffee, first."

The lines of her forehead relaxed despite having lost the battle. "You told me you're a novelist, but I haven't read anything by you. Have you published a novel?"

I was shocked by her unexpected question. I responded hesitantly, "That's true. I have a number of manuscripts, but the local publishing companies won't venture to publish the kinds of novels that I write."

"Why?"

"Quite simply, because in my novels I work on things that are not spoken of. So, I'm seriously thinking about publishing my latest novel in Beirut or Morocco. And I will probably submit it for the Naguib Mahfouz Medal for Literature."

This last statement was the only true one I uttered. During the past three years, I had exerted great effort in coming and going to the post office to make sure letters addressed to my post office box were arriving, but, unfortunately, "No one writes to the Colonel." Save one time when I got an honorable mention from the jury in a competition for science fiction. I was nineteenth on the list. That novel, which I ripped up without regret, revolves around a small planet that is hit by Halley's Comet and is turned to dust. All the inhabitants of this planet are giant ninja turtles. I think I wrote it at the time under the influence of the film *A Clockwork Orange* by Stanley Kubrick.

"I'd like to read your latest novel as soon as you finish writing it."

"It's still a first draft, but I've submitted what I've done to a typesetting office. There's another reason, though, stopping me from carrying out your request."

"What's that?"

"You are one of the protagonists of the novel."

"I am?"

"I'm sorry to say, yes."

"Sorry to say?"

"Because with a storm such as yourself, one can't ignore your powerful gusts, demolishing glass windows, electrical lines, and trees."

"Really?" she said joyfully, "That much? What have you written about me?"

"That's a secret."

"Please, I beg you. Tell me what you've written about me."

"Don't worry about it. Remember what al-Imam Muhammad Abduh said about novels, 'They are books of pure lies.'"

"You mean to say that you've written pure lies about me?"

"Something like that."

"Like what?" She panicked.

"Do you remember that sad kiss that was like a tragedy by Sophocles? I transformed it into fiery passion in the novel. But, what's really true is that I cannot forget the taste of cherry on your lips."

Then I added, with an invocation like a rain dance, "My dear Morning Glory, if you knew the extent of my passion for you, then you would crush my ribs without even touching them."

"So, I'm to understand from all these overtures that you love me, or in other words, you desire me. Is that it?" she said, cunningly.

"That's what your feminine intuition should tell you."

She shook her head silently then with a wit I wasn't familiar with said, "And where is this love heading, do you think?"

"To paths that do not end at the tower of desire."

"I'm assuming that the paths do end at the tower of desire. What's after that?"

"The gate of paradise, of course."

"You mean, marriage?"

With the horror of someone who has just taken a sip of spoiled soup, I answered, "Marriage! That's what they call the grave of love. That's not the gate of paradise for me. Anyway, two failed marriage experiences scared me straight, I made a pact to only marry the novel after that."

After a long silence on her part, I said, "Anyway, why rush the matter? Who knows, I may divorce the novel and marry you. If you imagine that all fruits ripen in the time it takes for strawberries to, then you certainly don't know anything about grapes."

I don't know from where I plucked this metaphor. Then, I ended my speech with a respected Hadith I'd worked hard to memorize, "Souls are like conscripted soldiers: those whom they recognize, they get along with, those whom they do not recognize, they do not."

"Let's leave it at that," she said. "I have a headache."

Paying the bill, I responded, "No doubt, it's heartache. It's an inevitable symptom of love rheumatism."

Out on the street, I immediately took her hand without any objection from her. At the first turn I wrapped my arm around her waist. We walked leisurely to Umayyad Square. I told her that I wanted to accompany her to make sure she got home safely, since it was now almost 10:30 at night.

Heading out to the suburb New Qadasiya in the microbus, I took the back seat. She sat facing the window connected to it. I placed my left hand on her knee. At any bump or jump of the bus, my hand would slip unintentionally up her thigh and then take advantage of her inability to protest because of a fat man sitting to my right. At Dummar Square she told me that she lives with a friend in a small apartment whose fiancé shows up sometimes. Her father died a few years ago and she misses her visits with her mother out in the countryside, but she has been finding it difficult to travel these days and so only makes it out there every two months.

I took the pen I bought for her out of my pocket. "So you remember me," I said. She took it happily and thanked me, squeezing her hand on mine in the darkness of the bus.

I prepared myself for tragedy, but as the bus approached the stop next to Morning Glory's house, she suddenly insisted I come in so that she could prepare coffee for me and I meet her friend Salwa. The apartment light was on. Ringing the bell, she said that perhaps Salwa was sleeping. She took a key from her bag and opened the door. I followed behind her. She stood in the hallway and turned on the living room light. "Please, come in." She headed for Salwa's room, returning almost immediately, "I guess she's not back yet."

I surveyed the layout of the small apartment. "What does Salwa do?" I asked.

"A nurse in a private hospital."

Hoping I was right, I said, "Perhaps she's on duty tonight."

"She didn't say anything." Then, "I'll go make the coffee."

I nodded my head and headed to the window overlooking the street from the second floor of the building to watch distant lights scattered on the mountaintop. Then I followed Morning Glory into the kitchen. I stood in the doorway, "I'd like to see your room."

She turned toward me, alarmed, "Please, no. I didn't clean it today."

"It doesn't matter. I just want to breathe in the scent of the pillow that nestles your silky hair every night."

"Wait a minute."

She carried the tray of coffee and set it on the table in the living room. Then she opened the door to her room. She began to straighten her things, which were scattered carelessly about, while I flipped through some of the sources she was using for her thesis. A candle in the shape of a red ball on the bedside table caught my attention. I took out my lighter and lit it.

"What are you doing?"

"Nothing," I said as I turned off the light.

She froze, confused. I approached her and clasped her cheeks in my palms, my fingers diving into the depths of her hair. "Please," she pleaded, "Salwa will be home any time."

"She's not coming. For sure, she is, right now, sitting with a patient, who won't die until dawn, and watching his IV."

"Let's drink coffee first."

"Your lips are tastier than any Brazilian bean."

Then I nibbled, sweetly, on her right ear. As I maneuvered down her neck, she tried to slip out of my hands.

Then I threw her down on the bed and kissed her on the lips. When the muscles of her face relaxed, I moved down to her neck and throat while my fingers massaged her shoulders under her woolen sweater, pushing her bra farther down to find her nipples and caress her flawless mounds.

When I lifted my head to her face, her eyes were almost closed, as if she were dreaming. I got up leisurely and went into the living room. I lit a cigarette and had a cup of coffee that tasted exceptionally good.

After about ten minutes, she called out for me in a feeble voice. I lit a second cigarette and headed to her. She was still stretched out on the bed and had covered her body with a red wool throw decorated with orange roses. I sat on the edge of the bed, playing with her hair. "Didn't I tell you that Salwa was on duty tonight?"

"And you're on duty with me."

Cunningly, I said, "I should go, it's getting late."

She grabbed my hand and pulled me under the cover. She was completely naked. I put out the candle and stretched out beside her. I was not sure, dreaming or awake? Now I knew what Shahrazad would say about being in a tight position: "If it were written by a needle in the corner of my eyes, then it would be a lesson for whoever takes heed." That I have suffered more horrors and difficulties than Sindbad the Sailor, who faced gale-force winds and storms on his journeys to the land of al-Waq Waq and unknown islands that no foot has ever alighted. I have tasted the fruit of trees I have never tasted before, and hope I will never have to leave this island. But as with any wonderful dream, it often ends with a nightmare. Morning Glory leapt up suddenly from the bed in a panic, "Salma's home. I hear her footsteps on the stairs."

We got dressed quickly, in a jumble befitting circus performers. Morning Glory went out first to scout out the scene. Meanwhile I took a seat at the table going over what Morning Glory had written so far on her thesis, jotting down frivolous and meaningless cryptic notes that looked like little birds, as if I were one of the characters in the judge al-Tannukhi's famous text *Happiness after Hardship*. According to the arrangement that my beloved had executed, she came in with Salwa in hand, and introduced me with deference and a pompous literary moniker that released some of the pressure, "The great novelist."

I got up from the behind the table and shook her hand warmly. She was much more beautiful than I expected; brown-skinned, thin, short curly hair, quite a wide mouth and olive green eyes that were breathtaking. She embodied the most delightful aspects of Lumia and Morning Glory together.

Despite feeling spent, a sudden desire to get to know Salwa awoke in me. She seemed like a woman with experience; that life had given her a few slaps in these trials. We moved into the living room while Morning Glory prepared more coffee. Salwa took out a pack of cigarettes and offered me one, commenting nonchalantly, as if we had known each other for a long time, "Morning Glory told me about you, but I expected you to be older." Winking, she went on, "By the way, I read *In Praise of the Stepmother* in one night at the hospital." Glancing toward the kitchen door, she whispered, "Morning Glory can't handle an injection like that. Some tranquilizers and antibiotics are enough for her."

Defeated, I said, "Your inference misses the mark."

Laughing, she replied, "I don't think so! Anyway, it's a great novel. You can pass them along to me if you don't mind, for when I'm on duty at the hospital. I don't have a hobby like knitting or crocheting like the others."

The taxi driver who picked me up was rather outgoing. In the darkness of night he told me, without introductions, about his adventures in nightclubs, trying his best to give me the impression that he has a good relationship with the gypsy singers whom he brings every night to some of the clubs scattered about al-Rabwa Road. Just taking a quick look at him from the corner of my eye, I could tell he was a pimp. I nodded my head and listened to the songs coming from his crappy tape recorder. At the entrance to Old Qadasiya, he turned to me and said, "We haven't introduced ourselves."

"Mario Vargas Llosa," I answered.

He was taken aback, "You're a foreigner?"

"Yes."

"You look Tunisian."

"My mother's French and my father's an immigrant."

He continued the rest of the way in silence. At the end of the Muhajarin line, I got out of the car and walked the rest of the way looking for a thread to weave Salwa into the fabric of my semi-finished novel, resolving to get rid of the chapter on death, the preliminary sketches for which I had laid out for technical and thematic reasons. Over the last three months I had collected hundreds of novels and sources on love, desire, and separation. These alone would need free time and patient reading. In particular and after a lot of effort, I finally got my hands on a rare copy of the text, *The Bride's Gift and the Souls' Pleasure*, by al-Imam al-Alamah Abi Abdullah Muhammad bin Ahmad al-Tijani. It is an edition of twenty-five chapters from books on the science of matrimony. Even though al-Tijani delves deeply into the bodily sciences, I still could not find anything in particular on the foot, except for a few lines of text and three verses of poetry by Ibn al-Rumi. What I really found strange is that the Arabs have designated over a hundred words for joy, but only have two for the foot. In the section on "Mentioning the Foot," al-Tijani states that "The most well-structured feet are those with a pliable leg-bone and whose phalanx and toes are long, the opposite of which is stubby. It is said that the foot that does not have an arch is 'flat-footed.'"

The legal scholar al-Tijani delves deeply into the unexplored territories of the female body, borrowing tools of the ancient archaeologists to search for some ancient castaway embedded in the foot and that is particular to the aesthetics of the body and the map of desire among Arabs. He delves courageously, venturing across cragged mountains to the extent one imagines that the ancient Arabs did not bother with any other science than matrimony. If they were content with that, then they were sufficiently proud. So al-Tijani selected the work of 1,134 texts on the temptation of the body and the gardens of delight without forgetting to mention that this book of his "is not a book for nighttime entertainment, but rather a book of science and speculation."

Al-Alamah Abu Abdullah Muhammad bin Abi al-Qasim al-Tijani spent the last ten years of his life writing this book. He finished it in the year AH 711, the year he died in Morocco. The manuscript has 223 folios. It can be found today at the Chester Beatty Library in Dublin copied by Muhammad bin Sulayman al-Malki. The first book copied from this manuscript goes back to the year AH 1301 and was printed by al-Sharqiya Publishing in Egypt with an unabridged introduction and an accentuated rhetoric that sounds like this:

How much I entrust the treasures of its truths from the precious gems of Hadiths that can cure the weak heart with its spring of paradise. Its bouquet is a mixture of spirits that heals every weak and injured being. It heals in the gardens of evening discussions on the ethics of traditions and the brilliance of al-Azhar. It emits the water of life that extends a lifetime of joy. And it pleases the eye, anointing with kohl to the glorious exploits of the most distinguished persons. Why is the vestige of this book almost obliterated, and the traces of its knowledge wiped out in a corner of oblivion? God has destined . . . .

I thought for a moment during my interlude with al-Imam al-Alamah al-Tijani to ask him about his relationship with intertextuality and the geology of writing. Once he sensed what I meant, he put down what he was doing, though he kept a grip on his quill after placing a line under the latest sentence so as not to lose his train of thought. He was in the midst of the section "On Buttocks." He said, "Life, itself, is based on intertextuality. For Earth revolves around by itself every day with its own mechanism and the Senses receive things with their own tools, so that we see, smell, touch, taste, and hear. But what differs each time is our perception in the face of the other, whether it is a body or an inanimate object."

I said, definitively, "This is true. Bakhtin said, 'There is no virgin word without another voice already inhabiting it.'"

He nodded his head and pointed to a flowering pomegranate tree that was drooping against the window, "When the Umayyads brought this pomegranate tree to Andalusia, it started to have another taste and another fragrance. Why? Because it is planted in some other soil, exposed to different winds, and caressed by other hands."

"It's a body, as well," I said.

"The body," he said, "is the magnet of the soul. Attraction is not enough. Its solitude is renewed each time in accordance with the power of the other's magnet. The kiss is granted, and so the nectar of the lips is refreshed." Then he recited these lines of poetry:

> Like chamomile in the morning drinking from its sky
> Above it fresh water, below it morning dew.

I left al-Imam's house a little after sunset. He was still copying his manuscript and I did not venture to ask him a question that had been eating away at me as I had sat with this pious scholar. I wanted to know where his personal experience rested within this grand discussion of the body's beauty. Was he merely a copyist who transfers texts without any concern for Roland Barthes, Umberto Eco, and Julia Kristeva's theories on this field and their modern critical discoveries? Even the pre-Islamic poets engaged with the oldest theory of intertextuality, that of 'poetic oppositions.' The mu'allaqa of Imru' al-Qays, for example: "Stop, let us cry for the memory of a beloved and a home." It is merely a text on absence, but it is the most famous lamiya qasida in the vast sea of Arabic poetry's history. There are qasidas that do not recount the crying over ruins that have become, without outshining Imru' al-Qays's innovations (that wanton king), figuratively the absent origins of an unknown text. What the scholars al-Tijani and Ibn Abd Rabbih al-Andalusi (during an unique era) have done is merely intertextuality within a geology of writing. Or, according to Roland Barthes, "One layer erected on another layer." Perhaps what was gnawing at me that evening as I approached the building of the typesetter where I had left the first draft of my novel was the ghost of Salwa, who, in her way, was another archaeological layer in my excavation. What gave me hope was that one does not discover gold with merely one strike of the pickax. The discovery of America entailed dozens of boats that drowned in the tyranny of the sea before Christopher Columbus was able to lead them to it.

I descended the three steps that lead to the office, rang the bell and waited. The door opened and the same woman to whom I had originally submitted the manuscript stood in front of me. Smiling, she said, "I'm sorry for the delay, I was just putting on some coffee." Walking behind her in the lobby, I replied, "No problem."

I noticed the office was completely empty. She invited me to sit in the waiting room, "Would you like a cup of coffee?" she asked. "Sure," I answered.

I sat looking at pictures hanging on the wall and the manuscripts on the shelves that took up an entire wall. All of a sudden the sound of music arose from the typesetting room at the same time as the young woman returned carrying a tray of coffee.

She handed me a coffee and I took out a pack of cigarettes from my jacket pocket. "Cigarette?" She took one. I lit it for her, and with a movement I have come to perfect, brushed her fingers with my hand.

"I finished your manuscript two days ago."

"You must not have much to do," I said. Then I asked her about the owner of the office.

"He's traveling."

"Were you able to decipher my handwriting?"

"No problem. Your handwriting is clear and quite beautiful. Is this the first novel you've written?"

"Yes," I said. "Did you like it?"

Hesitating, she said, "It piqued my curiosity, especially the character of Lumia."

Then I said, putting fattier bait on the hook, "For sure, Lumia exhausted me. I got totally lost in her maze."

"Is she a real person?"

Crossing my legs, I answered, "She's merely an imagined character. But as you well know, there's neither pure imagination nor absolute truth for novelists."

"Are you the protagonist?"

I smiled like a fox immediately after devouring an entire chicken, "In all humility, yes."

Looking me up and down, she said, "But aren't you afraid of scandal?"

"Scandal," I said dismissively.

"I mean what if Lumia reads the novel?"

"I don't think about that while writing. I was the character's prisoner more than the character was mine." After enough silence, I went on, "When Tolstoy wrote *Anna Karenina*, he didn't intend to make her out to be a spinster or a traitor. She was just following her heart. Unfortunately, for moralistic reasons distinct to the conscience and ethics of nineteenth-century Russia, she took her own life on the train tracks."

"I read that novel and liked it a lot," she said.

"Can I ask you something?" I enquired. "Do you write down personal things? Memories, for example?"

"Sometimes. Except they're not really memories, it's more like poetry."

"You mean creative, imaginative, right?"

"I guess."

"All writing, including the novel, is an imaginative life. At the same time it's incomplete incidents. The only thing the novelist must do is to clothe these incidents with more events and so on."

"Did you bring more sections of your novel?"

"No. They still need more revision. Even what you have is only a draft that needs reworking. Speaking of which, I may discover bigger secrets about Lumia's character or Morning Glory's."

Getting up, she said, "I'll get you the manuscript."

"I also need another copy on a disc, if that's possible."

"No problem, just a few minutes."

It would be deceptive if I said that I did not think about seducing her and joining her in the printing press room on the pretext of checking on how things were going, especially since the conditions for swooping down on her were favorable. But I pushed the idea aside, for fear of her unknown response, reverberating: "The most beautiful gazelle is the one we have not hunted yet." Salwa had completely taken over my mind, almost shutting down the road to Morning Glory. Though when it comes to Lumia, she had completely vanished from my memory, to the extent that I had even forgotten her features and scent.

Huda handed me an envelope that contained the manuscript and disc. I thanked her for the coffee, shook her hand, and left.

On the computer screen, I looked over the manuscript with both care and malevolence. I no longer had the slightest desire to review what I had written over the past few months. I felt that the joy of writing manifests itself at the moment of writing, at the moment of the madness of creativity, at the dismantling of all high and forbidden walls. I discovered that I had not written a novel, but rather a collection of novels or, more precisely, ideas for novels. When I stopped at the story of the Baghdadi trader and Yasmine Zad, I had completely neglected the environment that surrounded them, one that would span at least twenty years. It would be possible, quite simply, to follow the trail of this lover and his trials and tribulations from Baghdad to Damascus, to Persia, Samarkand, and Bukhari and Andalusia, ending in Damascus at that narrow alley where Yasmine Zad's house stands. Just like me, the protagonist of my novel was pursuing a delusion or a mirage, never arriving at any kind of certainty. And for this reason, perhaps, I was searching for an impossible story. A story that has no end. A story that does not reveal its secret, like a traveler wandering in the desert without any association to guide him to a water well. As soon as he gets closer to the object of his search, he discovers that it is only a mirage and that the one tangible truth he has is that he will die of thirst and there is no way to quench it in this perilous desert except with "the love of life."

I was really at pains to bring this novel writing to an end, to leave my characters, friends, scribes, copyists, and artists. But the more I became conscious that I should stop, the more I could feel my chest pound and my lungs compress, the more I felt that life as a whole had no meaning.

I turned off the computer and was stricken by anxiety as to the fate of these quiescent characters within the confines of pages made up of disparate times as they searched for some certainty to protect themselves from destruction. I got up from the computer and picked up the phone with the intention of calling Salwa at the hospital. But, without thinking, I dialed Lumia's number. Perhaps under the effect of sudden desire.

Despite all the defeats between us, I could not forget her scent, those roaring nights, and heated discussions that would end with a laugh reverberating from her and an inscrutable acknowledgment on my side that perhaps "I had fallen in love with her, with a madness that ignores all the acute contradictions between us." I heard her spent voice, "Hello?"

"I miss you," I said.

"Is that possible?"

"I myself find it strange to be in this position suddenly."

"Go find someone else to practice your soft side on, I'm no longer suitable for the role."

"But I miss you, really."

"I'm talking to you from Sidnaya, where we are shooting."

"When are you coming back?"

"Not before three in the morning."

"May God answer your prayers."

Once again, I wanted to dial Salwa's number, but something indefinable stopped me from doing so. I felt that Salwa, though I had only just met her, would be the one to destroy my life. And so it follows, she would destroy my novel. But it was impossible for me to ignore her presence and the scent of her acrid skin even though I had not yet touched her. But initial indications support the feeling that her path is paved and there will not be any pitfalls or roadblocks in my way as I promenade in the garden of her infernal labyrinth.

Throughout this time, I was ignoring Morning Glory's presence, pushing her away from the screen of my imagination and considering what happened between a mere printing error that ought to be corrected straight away. Indeed, whoever nests in the delusions of *Broken Wings* will certainly not meet up with one who soars in the vast spaces of bodily texts and acknowledge my depravity with her. Indeed my relationship with her was merely the seduction of a rabbit scared of approaching the carrot of disobedience. I had even inadvertently named it the carrot of stormy desire. It was up to her alone to find a solution to her problem, if we assume that what happened between us is a problem. I reassured her at our first encounter after that stormy night that she should let fate take our boat to unknown shores, and that it was too early to think about a dry end for our wonderful story of crazy love.

I gave her a little advice about madness, that it was a curative antidote for all delicate illnesses. I also shamelessly exaggerated the development of her style in coming closer to a subject for her master's thesis and assured her that opening the flowers of her body played an influential role in determining intrinsic points that were absent from her research on narrative in the contemporary novel. Of course, she was not pleased with my advice because, in case I did not mention it earlier, I had in fact crashed into Ibn Hazm, who was sitting in front of her. She wore his facial features, the wisdom of Ibn Sina, and the rational intellect of Ibn Rushd all at the same time.

In order to ease her frustration, I told her, "It was truly a crazy night." Then I added with a clear nonchalance, "What's going on with your friend Salwa?"

She replied, calmly, "She advised me to stay away from you."

"And how does she justify such stupid advice?"

"She doesn't. It's just a feeling that we won't stay together."

"Have you told her anything about what happened between us?"

"She figured it out herself, which made me confess what happened that night."

"Do you regret it?"

"No, but I didn't imagine that you would get rid of me this easily and so indifferently."

"I never said I'd get rid of you. But I don't like being shackled, and I refuse to be a part of a love fraught with conditions and promises I may not be able to keep."

"There's no need to distort matters," she replied. "What I liked about you was your forthrightness and compassion. You were sweet with me all the time."

I replied with a shameful and transparent depravity, "And I will continue to be sweet with you because I can't forget you. You are a wound that has never and will never heal in my life."

"I'm thinking about going to my village tomorrow or the day after."

"How long will you be away?"

"I don't know, a week or more."

"In this condition, I ought to say goodbye another way."

Rebuking me, she said, "Thanks. Your services to me won't be forgotten."

She grabbed her bag off the back of the chair and got up. "Wait, I'll take you to the bus stop." I said.

"Thanks, but I'm taking a taxi."

I said goodbye to her on the curb next to the café. I could not disregard the sad look she threw at me from behind the car window. As the taxi moved away, I raised my hand to wave and sensed a drizzle of rain that felt like spit wetting my face.

I stood for a few moments in place, not sure of what to do. Where should I head? I walked, my steps disordered, up al-Mutanabbi Street and stopped in front of al-Yaqza Bookstore. The storefront was filled with books, political memoirs, books on military coups, books on Bedouin, and some new titles on the war in Afghanistan, with pictures of Bin Laden in his well-known outfit and long black beard adorning their covers. I right away thought about a news report—I had cut it out of one of the papers—that surveilled details of the greatest carnage that a library has ever been subjected to in the twentieth century. On 12 August 1998 the Taliban set out to burn the contents of the national library in Kabul using Soviet-made weaponry in half the wings of the library, annihilating and burning 5,005 volumes—some of them rare. And this was before the decision to devastate and destroy the ancient artifacts in the National Museum outside Kabul, and after that, the infamous dynamiting of the Buddha sculptures of Bamiyan, unique in size and craftsmanship. I said to myself, "The entire world wants to destroy memory, and here I am wanting to revisit and restore it."

The most agonizing aspect of my predicament was how to draw the final map of my characters' destinies: Lumia, Morning Glory, and Salwa. I was thrust by an irresistible desire to animate Salwa's character more definitively. She was the one I had not worked on as I should have, because she had entered my world suddenly, without any previous planning on my part. I thought about a way of getting rid of her, but in no time I retreated under the pressure of a mysterious sensation that she had a password like no other. She is the only apple tree in an orchard whose fruit I have not tasted. In stories, there is always a closed room that the narrator is advised not to enter because it leads to hell and means leaving the castle's garden forever. With drunken encouragement, I picked up the telephone and called her, making sure it had been at least two days since Morning Glory's last call. I heard her sweet and arousing voice, "Hello."

"I want to see you," I said.

With an even more arousing tone that immediately made me hot, she replied, "It's late."

"I haven't forgotten you since I saw you that night."

"Be careful." She answered, "You're talking to Salwa, not Morning Glory."

"My temperature's up and I need a quick injection from the most beautiful nurse in the world. Yours is the only number I found in the phone book."

After three bottles of German beer, Salwa confessed all her frustrations and disappointments. She said, "I wasn't surprised when you called me. I expected it." Continuing, "I have a strong sense of smell and I knew that you would stray as soon as opportunity knocked, looking for salvation. I decided the first time I saw you to water the drought that's inside you."

The music in the bar that Salwa chose was roaring. I felt defeated in front of her. I said, "I don't like loud music. What do you say we leave here?"

"Whatever you want."

We walked arm-in-arm down narrow, semi-dark alleys. She walked a bit uneasily. I stopped a taxi and we got in to the back seat in silence. I took her hand and played with her palm. I told the driver, "To al-Abyad Bridge." She looked at me submissively, causing more unrest in me. I felt like I was in a rosy dream.

As soon as we got to my place, she said, "Do you have anything to drink?"

"There's some wine," I replied.

She nodded her head in agreement. After taking a big sip from her glass, she lit a Hamra cigarette: "I'm not a fallen woman, like you might think. But over time, I've learned how to give my body what it wants." Continuing, "At work in the hospital I resisted innumerable passes from doctors and nurses. I vigorously resisted. But, at night, when I would dive into bed, I would evoke a body that could seduce me and I would engage it with pleasure. And when that pleasure turned into a habit, I abstained and agreed to an unofficial marriage to a doctor who worked the same shifts as me. When I discovered he was gay, I ripped up the marriage document and spit in his face. And from that day on I started to follow my body's inclinations."

She emptied her glass and lay her head on her knees.

I moved closer and sat next to her. She lifted her face toward me and I hugged her with sudden emotion, feeling as if I needed to cry. I slumped over her shoulder like a small rag. After about ten minutes of complete silence, she caressed my shoulder warmly. I lifted my head with the distress of a sailor who had lost his life preserver. I gave her room so she could get up. Smiling victoriously, she said, "We'll meet again, for sure." I nodded in surrender. I followed her to the door. She granted me a quick kiss and left.

I returned to my chair, totally bewildered by what had stricken me and not believing what had happened. For a terrifying moment, I thought I was dreaming, but then noticed, on the couch facing me where Salwa was sitting, a small, metal object made of silver. Looking at it closely, I realized it was a part of an earring. It must have slipped off her ear. It was in the shape of a triangle with delicate lacework, the Latin letter *S* in the middle. It looked like a Chinese hand-held fan. I took it as a good omen.

I got up from my seat and sat in front of the computer screen excited. "I will write, propelled by the joy of narrative. It is the human condition that is most like flying," as Marquez once said, without my thinking where life ends and imagination begins.

Like celestial inspiration, the title of my novel, which had mostly given me insomnia during the days of writing, came to me. I wrote it on the first page, which was still white, without the slightest fear or hesitation: *Writing Love.*

Glossary

Antar wa Abla A popular epic poem that recounts the adventures and hardships of the real-life pre-Islamic hero–poet Antara, who overcame his low status to become a leader and marry his beloved Abla.

Dhu al-Qa'da The eleventh month of the Islamic calendar.

Farid al-Atrash (1910–74) Syrian–Egyptian composer, oud player, and singer. He was born in Suwayda, Syria, but his family moved to Egypt to escape the French occupation. Beloved for his voice, al-Atrash starred in over thirty Egyptian films. On stage, he would always improvise a few poetic lines, in the style of *mawal,* a traditional genre that is sung in colloquial rather than classical Arabic.

fuul Stewed fava beans. An inexpensive staple food, often served with tahini or olive oil.

Hafiz al-Shirazi (d. circa 1325) Persian lyric poet, often referred to simply as 'Hafiz' (meaning someone who has memorized the Quran). It is said that he only composed poetry when he was divinely inspired, many lines of his poetry still serving as the basis for proverbs and sayings.

Hanna Mina (1924–) a prominent Syrian novelist who wrote works of social realism.

Ibn Hazm (d. 1064) Muslim theologian and man of letters born in Cordoba, most famous for his treatise on love and lovers, "The Ring of the Dove."

al-Jahiz (d. circa 869) Prolific writer of literary prose, Mu'tazilite theology, and political polemics, born in Basra, but who lived most of his adult life in Baghdad, writing under the patronage of the Abbasid court. His name, al-Jahiz, literally means 'boggle-eyed.'

Jalal al-Din al-Rumi (d. 1273) Sufi poet, philosopher, theologian, and mystic, born in Persia. Among his numerous writings, he is remembered most popularly for his poetry. Also known as Mevlana in Turkey and Mawlana in Iran and Afghanistan.

***Kalila wa Dimna* by Ibn al-Muqaffa'** Arabic translation (735 CE) from the Persian of the ancient Indian *Panchatantra*, by Ibn al-Muqaffa', a Persian man of letters, who lived in Basra and worked for the Abbasids. It is a collection of animal fables within a frame story that teach moral and other life lessons. These stories have been collected and retold for centuries throughout the world and continue to be transmitted to this day.

Majnun Layla A popular epic story of unrequited love often told in verse and based on a real-life 'Majnun' (mad, crazy one) who falls in love with Layla, but is forbidden to marry her.

maqama (pl. maqamat) A form of Arabic rhymed prose believed to have been developed by al-Hamadhani in the tenth century. Told by a narrator, the *maqama* relates the travels and exploits of a protagonist–trickster in decorated prose, and often became the basis for lexicographic and rhetorical studies (especially those by al-Hamadhani's successor al-Hariri in the eleventh century).

mu'allaqa Literally, 'the hanging one.' Refers to seven long poems (*qasida*s) that were hung on the Ka'ba in Mecca in pre-Islamic days. Widely revered, these poems are seen as a high point of pre-Islamic literature and formed the structural basis for classical Arabic poetry for centuries to follow.

nay A wind instrument.

Nizar Qabbani (1923–98) Syrian poet known for his romantic and love poems, many of which form the basis of popular Arabic songs. He later turned to writing socially and politically engaged poetry, particularly after the Arab defeat in the 1967 war with Israel.

qasida, lamiya qasida A qasida is a classical Arabic ode poem that contains a single meter and rhyming scheme throughout. It is typically long (more than fifty lines) and is usually formed in three parts: a nostalgic opening; a release or disengagement, often giving an account of travel; and the 'message' of the poem. The *lamiya qasida* refers to a collection of such poems, in which the rhyme falls on the final letter, in this case the *lam*.

qayna (pl. qiyan) A singing slave girl.

Saga of al-Amira Dhat al-Himma (*see* ***Antar wa Abla***) Epic oral poem, like the *Antara wa Abla* cycle, in this case relating the exploits and wonders of a princess.

saj bread A kind of flatbread, common to the Levant, traditionally baked in a wood-burning oven.

Samia Gamal, Fifi Abdou Two famous Egyptian belly dancers and actresses.

Su'ad al-Sabah Prize Cultural and literary prizes awarded by Kuwaiti poet Su'ad al-Sabah (1942–).

al-Tijani Fourteenth-century Tunisian jurisprudent.

Umayyad Mosque Constructed on the site of the basilica of St. John the Baptist in Damascus after the conquest of the city in 634 CE. It is one of the oldest and largest mosques in the world, and is considered the fourth holiest site in Islam. It contains the tomb of Salah al-Din (Saladin) and a shrine that is said to contain the head of St. John.

Modern Arabic Literature
from the American University in Cairo Press

Bahaa Abdelmegid *Saint Theresa* and *Sleeping with Strangers*
Ibrahim Abdel Meguid *Birds of Amber* • *Distant Train*
No One Sleeps in Alexandria • *The Other Place*
Yahya Taher Abdullah *The Collar and the Bracelet* • *The Mountain of Green Tea*
Leila Abouzeid *The Last Chapter*
Hamdi Abu Golayyel *A Dog with No Tail* • *Thieves in Retirement*
Yusuf Abu Rayya *Wedding Night*
Ahmed Alaidy *Being Abbas el Abd*
Idris Ali *Dongola* • *Poor*
Rasha al Ameer *Judgment Day*
Radwa Ashour *Granada* • *Specters*
Ibrahim Aslan *The Heron* • *Nile Sparrows*
Alaa Al Aswany *Chicago* • *Friendly Fire* • *The Yacoubian Building*
Fadhil al-Azzawi *Cell Block Five* • *The Last of the Angels*
The Traveler and the Innkeeper
Ali Bader *Papa Sartre*
Liana Badr *The Eye of the Mirror*
Hala El Badry *A Certain Woman* • *Muntaha*
Salwa Bakr *The Golden Chariot* • *The Man from Bashmour* • *The Wiles of Men*
Halim Barakat *The Crane*
Hoda Barakat *Disciples of Passion* • *The Tiller of Waters*
Mourid Barghouti *I Saw Ramallah* • *I Was Born There, I Was Born Here*
Mohamed Berrada *Like a Summer Never to Be Repeated*
Mohamed El-Bisatie *Clamor of the Lake* • *Drumbeat* • *Hunger* • *Over the Bridge*
Mahmoud Darwish *The Butterfly's Burden*
Tarek Eltayeb *Cities without Palms* • *The Palm House*
Mansoura Ez Eldin *Maryam's Maze*
Ibrahim Farghali *The Smiles of the Saints*
Hamdy el-Gazzar *Black Magic*
Randa Ghazy *Dreaming of Palestine*
Gamal al-Ghitani *Pyramid Texts* • *The Zafarani Files* • *Zayni Barakat*
Tawfiq al-Hakim *The Essential Tawfiq al-Hakim*
Yahya Hakki *The Lamp of Umm Hashim*
Abdelilah Hamdouchi *The Final Bet*
Bensalem Himmich *The Polymath* • *The Theocrat*
Taha Hussein *The Days*
Sonallah Ibrahim *Cairo: From Edge to Edge* • *The Committee* • *Zaat*
Yusuf Idris *City of Love and Ashes* • *The Essential Yusuf Idris*
Denys Johnson-Davies *The AUC Press Book of Modern Arabic Literature*
Homecoming • *In a Fertile Desert* • *Under the Naked Sky*
Said al-Kafrawi *The Hill of Gypsies*
Mai Khaled *The Magic of Turquoise*
Sahar Khalifeh *The End of Spring*
The Image, the Icon and the Covenant • *The Inheritance* • *Of Noble Origins*
Edwar al-Kharrat *Rama and the Dragon* • *Stones of Bobello*
Betool Khedairi *Absent*

Mohammed Khudayyir *Basrayatha*
Ibrahim al-Koni *Anubis* • *Gold Dust* • *The Puppet* • *The Seven Veils of Seth*
Naguib Mahfouz *Adrift on the Nile* • *Akhenaten: Dweller in Truth*
Arabian Nights and Days • *Autumn Quail* • *Before the Throne* • *The Beggar*
The Beginning and the End • *Cairo Modern* • *The Cairo Trilogy: Palace Walk*
Palace of Desire • *Sugar Street* • *Children of the Alley* • *The Coffeehouse*
The Day the Leader Was Killed • *The Dreams* • *Dreams of Departure*
Echoes of an Autobiography • *The Essential Naguib Mahfouz* • *The Final Hour*
The Harafish • *Heart of the Night* • *In the Time of Love*
The Journey of Ibn Fattouma • *Karnak Cafe* • *Khan al-Khalili* • *Khufu's Wisdom*
Life's Wisdom • *Love in the Rain* • *Midaq Alley* • *The Mirage* • *Miramar* • *Mirrors*
Morning and Evening Talk • *Naguib Mahfouz at Sidi Gaber* • *Respected Sir*
Rhadopis of Nubia • *The Search* • *The Seventh Heaven* • *Thebes at War*
The Thief and the Dogs • *The Time and the Place* • *Voices from the Other World*
Wedding Song • *The Wisdom of Naguib Mahfouz*
Mohamed Makhzangi *Memories of a Meltdown*
Alia Mamdouh *The Loved Ones* • *Naphtalene*
Selim Matar *The Woman of the Flask*
Ibrahim al-Mazini *Ten Again*
Yousef Al-Mohaimeed *Munira's Bottle* • *Wolves of the Crescent Moon*
Hassouna Mosbahi *A Tunisian Tale*
Ahlam Mosteghanemi *Chaos of the Senses* • *Memory in the Flesh*
Shakir Mustafa *Contemporary Iraqi Fiction: An Anthology*
Mohamed Mustagab *Tales from Dayrut*
Buthaina Al Nasiri *Final Night*
Ibrahim Nasrallah *Inside the Night* • *Time of White Horses*
Haggag Hassan Oddoul *Nights of Musk*
Mona Prince *So You May See*
Mohamed Mansi Qandil *Moon over Samarqand*
Abd al-Hakim Qasim *Rites of Assent*
Somaya Ramadan *Leaves of Narcissus*
Kamal Ruhayyim *Days in the Diaspora*
Mahmoud Saeed *The World through the Eyes of Angels*
Mekkawi Said *Cairo Swan Song*
Ghada Samman *The Night of the First Billion*
Mahdi Issa al-Saqr *East Winds, West Winds*
Rafik Schami *The Calligrapher's Secret* • *Damascus Nights* • *The Dark Side of Love*
Habib Selmi *The Scents of Marie-Claire*
Khairy Shalaby *The Hashish Waiter* • *The Lodging House*
Khalil Sweileh *Writing Love*
The Time-Travels of the Man Who Sold Pickles and Sweets
Miral al-Tahawy *Blue Aubergine* • *Brooklyn Heights* • *Gazelle Tracks* • *The Tent*
Bahaa Taher *As Doha Said* • *Love in Exile*
Fuad al-Takarli *The Long Way Back*
Zakaria Tamer *The Hedgehog*
M. M. Tawfik *Murder in the Tower of Happiness*
Mahmoud Al-Wardani *Heads Ripe for Plucking*
Amina Zaydan *Red Wine*
Latifa al-Zayyat *The Open Door*